Totally Bound Publishing books by Landra Graf

Bad Boys of Space
A Talent for Trouble
A Gamble Among Sheep
The Body Collector
A Mercenary to Love

Full Throttle Cyborgs
Snap Me Up

Full Throttle Cyborgs

JACK THIS HEART

LANDRA GRAF

Jack This Heart
ISBN # 978-1-80250-996-0
©Copyright Landra Graf 2022
Cover Art by Erin Dameron-Hill ©Copyright November 2022
Interior text design by Claire Siemaszkiewicz
Totally Bound Publishing

Published in 2022 by Totally Bound Publishing, United Kingdom.

JACK THIS
HEART

Dedication

To Sherry T. for my introduction to K-Dramas.

Chapter One

The rush of the wind, the scent of iron-rich dirt in the air, and the vibration tingling the pads of his fingertips — Jack Renfro had missed all these things. Add in the way his cyborg foot could put the pedal to the metal, and sitting behind the wheel of the new Full Throttle racer was the comeback he'd been waiting for.

They'd rebuilt the racer in less than a month after the explosion...the damn explosion that had taken appendages from his fellow driver, Hemi. An explosion with a victim, but no guilty party located.

Bastards.

Jack gritted his teeth as he slowly turned the wheel coming out of turn two on the track, loving the feel of the ground under the tires. This racer handled like a dream, and while he despised the circumstances that got him behind the wheel again, he couldn't deny the immense pleasure coursing through his veins.

The test drive today was all about his control of the speed, the angles. They'd upgrade to running against obstacles in the next couple days. But if he passed this handling portion, he'd ask if he could trigger the NiteOx, or nitrous oxide in scientific terms. The liquid mixture ignited with the Marsanium sludge to create a faster burning fuel mix, which would allow him to speed up even more on the track. That same chemical compound had ruined his future, but circumstances were different now. Full Throttle had an engineer and mechanics team light-years past the competition his old gang, the Smiths, had supplied.

Dust or bust.

This had been Jack's life prior to the accident. He'd been the top racer for the Smith gang-town. Then there had been the explosion from a new test engine—he'd lost his leg and his shot at a championship. He'd been lost for a bit after the crash, unsure of his future and whether life was worth living. The cybernetic test had given him another chance. No way would he screw it up.

Not this time.

No, he'd get this baby up to speed and past those barriers holding both him and the racer back. Even now, coming out of turn three, the racer was the perfect balance of tight and loose.

"Gina, you and Snapper really worked a miracle on this one. I'm about to hit top-out speeds. On the next straightaway, am I clear to trigger?" The moment of truth—he waited it out. The buzz in his ears was a mixture of the background static in his helmet communicator and the stupid hum of the engine roar as he started to come out of the last turn.

"If you feel she's ready, you're a go." Snapper's response came through with confidence in his tone.

The trust Jack picked up surged through him. They were leaving this in his hands, and damn it if he wouldn't make them proud. For once in his life, he'd finally exceed beyond where he'd come from. He'd be more than the son of the town addict and her lovelorn sucker of a husband.

The shining metal of his cyborg foot glimmered as the sun's rays reflected off it, the pressure on the gas pedal lessening. A sharp pain jolted into his right hip and Jack did his best not to jerk the wheel, especially when the pain spread. He had to release his hold on the pedal entirely.

The racer began to reduce in speed. No more wind. No more blur of the stands. No more testing.

"Jack, what the hell is happening out there?"

He could hear Snapper's question echo, along with Gina's repeated concerns in the background. But all he could get out in response was, "Help. It hurts."

* * * *

"Bullshit!" Jack snatched the holo-tablet from the doctor's hands and threw it across the room.

"I'm charging Full Throttle for that," the doctor replied as he resituated his glasses on the bridge of his nose. His lips were in a flat line, arms crossed in displeasure.

"You're being ridiculous, Jack. Hear what the man has to say." Gina, with a swing of her blonde ponytail, leaned down and picked up the tablet. She brought it back over and set it on the side of the bed. Right next to Jack's offensive cybernetic appendage.

"What's there to hear? I'm defective, again. First, I didn't have a leg. Now the one I have has turned out to be a dud."

"You're not defective, just not approved to race." The doctor's face was solemn as he gave Jack the verdict that nailed his death pod shut. And Full Throttle's.

"What would change your mind?" Jack asked.

This was a commission doctor, since the accident had happened on the racing track...meaning his findings would be reported to the commission. Once filed, Jack wouldn't be able to get around them.

Drag, their gang leader, would be unable to replace him with another racer. The stupid rules only allowed for one replacement if the winning champion couldn't race.

The doctor cocked one bushy gray eyebrow. "Are you trying to bribe me?"

Snapper, their lead engineer, who had been sitting in a corner chair flexing and clenching his cybernetic fingers over and over, jolted out of his seat. "No, not at all. Not a bribe. What's it gonna cost to fix this?"

The doc shrugged. "No idea. Afraid I know nothing about your cybernetic components that make me any help in this situation. You're best to go to the original physician who thought it a genius idea to give you these parts to begin with."

"And if we don't even know who that is?" Jack asked, more than annoyed. He wanted to throw a few more things or take a hacksaw to this useless piece of equipment attached to him.

The doctor stood up, pulling at the lapels of his stained jacket. He raised both those bushy eyebrows then gave a ridiculously loud scoff. "Well, I can't help idiots who willingly submit to experimentation without all the details. I'll report his status to the commission" — this was directed to Snapper — "If something changes, you can bring him back and I'll evaluate him again. Currently, whatever technology is operating that leg is degrading, and the lack of control over the limb, along with his pain, will worsen with time. I can't tell you how long, so don't bother asking. Your best bet is to get your original champion back in the racer so you don't lose your spot."

Jack growled. "If we needed your opinion on what's best for our gang-town and the championship, we would have—"

"Thanks for all your help, doctor. We'll bring him back when we get him all straightened up." Gina's words and her hand clapped over his mouth stopped him short.

He tried to free himself from her hand, but she had more strength than any of them, being the first-ever synthetic human. More knowledge too, but he didn't appreciate being silenced.

The doctor gave a single nod, then exited the room they were in within the racing track's bowels.

"I'm going to let go of you now, but you don't get to say anything until I tell you it's safe. Nod once if you agree. If you don't, I'll knock you out now and have Snapper carry you to the hauler."

Jack gave a single nod and Gina stepped away.

She glanced at Snapper. "You drive the racer back to Frog Lick and I'll drive Jack."

"Give me the decency—"

"Ah, I meant what I said, Jack. One more outburst and chokehold it is."

Snapper grinned. "I wanna see that."

Jack frowned. He had so many things he wanted to say in response. But he kept silent because ultimately he was jealous of what they had, of something so pure. The support between them, the love… He had nothing to offer at the moment but negativity and he didn't want to be knocked out only for others in their gang to find out about his condition, either.

"We can coordinate with Drag when we get back. But the rules are correct—we were only allowed one replacement option. Jack wasn't officially submitted... yet."

Shit... He didn't want to lose this chance.

Full Throttle needed to win the championship. They couldn't put the pressure back on Hemi. He was still getting used to having not one, but two cybernetic limbs, a chest plate and at least four ribs. He was more machine than the rest of them.

"We could always reach back out to Sampson for that cybernetic expert he brought in from the moon." Snapper ran a hand through his hair then shrugged. "I mean, if they could fix Hemi, maybe."

They were thinking the same things. *Good, maybe this will still work out.*

"Jack, you can speak now."

Finally. "I'm with Snapper. It's a solid idea. He might be able to fix this."

Gina nodded. "It's worth a try. In the meantime, we can talk to Hemi's nurse. She's a cybernetic expert in her own right. She was involved in Kascade's original plans from the get-go. That's why she was recommended to us by Sampson. We're lucky we found her already on Mars."

"Anyone but her." Jack let out a groan, then moved his leg to try to mask his disgust as pain.

"You don't like her? I can't see pain receptors firing in your leg, Jack. Don't try to bullshit me."

Snapper walked up and wrapped his arms around his woman. "I love you, you know that, right?"

Jack groaned. "Can we keep the smooching and cuddling to a minimum?"

Snapper pressed his lips to Gina's, then gave Jack a pointed look. "No."

"Fine. The answer is I don't like the nurse…Sharon, Susan."

"Shannon."

Jack snapped his fingers. "Yep, that's the one. She's condescending, annoying. That laugh of hers is somewhere between the wailing cry of a goosemert and the cackle of one of those hyenas the Singh gang-town got for guard dogs."

"Never knew you to be so discriminatory toward a lady's response to humor… Hell, didn't know if you bothered to make them laugh. You always worked on the swooning, flirting thing."

"Shut up, Snapper. Before I try to work those same wiles on your woman."

Gina grinned up at Snapper. "It'd never work. I'm all yours, baby."

"Can I go to the hauler already? I don't need to be carried. I think I can walk."

That got both of their attention. Gina was the first to pull away and Snapper took that as his signal to head out of the room, no doubt for the racer.

"If you think you can, then let's do it. I'll be here every step of the way if something goes wrong."

Jack sighed and tried to let his anger out with his exhale. "I'm not a kid."

"And you're not exactly one hundred percent. It's okay to need help, Jack. Let me do this, and I can talk to Shannon."

It was funny how Gina acted like she was asking him. He damn well knew she'd talk to Drag and their fearless leader would let her do whatever she thought best. Since she'd single-handedly designed the racer that had gotten them their first success, her opinions mattered to everyone. Even if Jack hated this particular view.

"Like I have a choice in the matter."

She grinned and stood at the ready as he pushed himself up off of the bed. "No, you don't. But it sounds far better than me saying you'll do as I say or else. Humor me, and if something goes wrong, it will be my fault."

Therein lay the problem... Something had already gone wrong. This would just be the bonus bullshit to his continuing streak of bad luck.

Chapter Two

"Just lift and hold." Shannon directed Hemi from her seat across the way from him. This makeshift physical training room the Full Throttle gang had outfitted proved they cared far more for their people than Shannon's own family ever had.

Once upon a time... The past doesn't determine my future.

Hemi let out a grunt of frustration as he tried to hold his metal cybernetic leg aloft, sweat beads gathered on his forehead. "If it's so easy, how about you do it, too?"

Shannon stuck both her legs out in front of her, using her hands to brace her weight on the chair, and lifted straight up. "Got any more challenges for me? Give it ten more seconds. Count down with me."

They spoke the numbers out loud, the echo of their voices reflecting off the metal walls with the wooden frame. Another part of these Wespero territory gang-towns she'd found interesting — they built houses, stores, mechanics bays. They kept all their possessions above ground. Odd, and far more trusting than any other gang-town she'd visited in the Auster territory region of Mars. Those gangs found strength in hiding their wealth from prying eyes.

"You can lower now."

Hemi followed her direction and took a few deep breaths before wiping his face with the rag on his lap. "Do you think it will get any easier?"

He'd asked her this question before, back when he'd first started working with her on the physical therapy to gain use of his new cybernetic appendages. The racing accident he'd experienced hadn't just cost him an arm and a leg, but his confidence.

Some scars dig deeper.

"I don't know. Guess it depends on how hard you work. I imagine you'll always feel different, but you're still you."

"Really?" Hemi cocked a grin at her. "Then let me buy you a drink tonight."

"Are you really flirting with your healthcare professional?"

He shrugged and readjusted himself in the chair. "Maybe... That's part of who I was once, the flirt. I mean, don't lie—what chance do I have with any woman now? They all think I'm a freak."

Shannon opened her mouth, prepared to ask him who'd called him names, when the main door creaked open.

"Hemi, you're as gorgeous as the day I met you. Definitely not a freak," Gina said as she walked into the room, past the tool chest and table they'd set up with various wheels, hammers, blocks and other objects to be used for weightlifting. The woman was tall and lithe, with blonde hair that fell in a long ponytail to her ass. She was gorgeous and everything opposite of Shannon.

"You're saying that because you feel guilty."

Shannon hadn't been briefed on all the details of what had caused the crash, but she knew the extent of Hemi's injuries. That was what she'd been hired for — to care for this man who'd been taken apart and put together, like some old Earth rhyme.

Dumpty Rumpty.

Gina reached them and placed a hand on Hemi's cybernetic shoulder. "Guilt has nothing to do with anything. I only feel frustration that we haven't located the person who rigged..."

She trailed off as his gaze tracked over to Shannon.

The only downside to being an outsider in this gang-town was censored conversation. Shannon would've been rich if she got a gold leaf every time someone halted or stuttered over their words around her. Afraid to speak of 'gang' business or confess some sort of secret.

"Racers don't typically blow up unless someone rigged them to. You don't have to hide whatever you want to say from me." Shannon ran a finger over her lips, imitating sealing them shut. "I'm a locked box."

"But you're not Full Throttle."

Shannon almost rolled her eyes at Gina's response. How many ridiculous times had she heard such a statement? *Too many.*

Every gang-town across Mars disliked outsiders. Shannon could easily proclaim she didn't belong to anyone or anything.

And I don't fucking want to.

Twice she'd made the mistake of believing in something — in the idea that she belonged somewhere — though the second time she'd been wise enough to see the end coming before it hit. She'd barely escaped the Humans First movement without getting caught by the Upper Pup units. A future where she'd have been locked in a Saturn rings jail cell, her bones marked for powder production.

Instead, she'd slipped into the ether, eking out an existence in the wilds of Mars, bouncing from gang-town to gang-town and using her knowledge of anatomy and cybernetics to do it, among her other talents.

"Hemi, do you mind if I talk to Shannon for a minute?"

He glanced in Shannon's direction and she appreciated how he sought her approval to end their session early.

She gave a little nod.

Hemi pushed himself out of the chair and flexed his hands, though the cybernetic reaction was a little slower than Shannon would have liked. He gave a good stroke to his bushy black beard and sighed. "I'm off to the hole for a drink then."

"Be by early tomorrow. I want to do some strength and input tests for your arm and hand." Regardless of her true motives, she wanted to ensure she left Hemi in a better place than when she'd been brought in.

I didn't do enough for the first group.

"Sure, sure." He hollered over his shoulder as he walked toward the exit, "If you want me to take my clothes off too, that can be negotiated."

"And we'll talk about the flirting."

The door slammed shut behind him,

"Do those lines really work?" she asked Gina, who sat down in the metal folding chair Hemi had vacated.

"I don't know. Afraid I'm too much of a working girl—wait, that's the wrong word. I'm too focused on my work, that's it. I don't pay attention to what the others do unless it involves racing."

This Gina was an odd duck, incredibly smart and with a knack for hearing things most wouldn't pick up and seeing things others wouldn't notice. Shannon figured she was harmless in general, though no amount of kindness extended to the woman got her any closer to the Full Throttle mechanics bay.

"I wanted to talk to you about—"

"Hemi's progress."

Gina shook her head. "No, from what I can tell, he's improved a lot since you started helping, though he has a way to go. But he's walking and capable of basic function. More than we could have hoped for. This is about an opportunity to help out Full Throttle."

Perfect, the *in* Shannon had been looking for. The sooner she gained access to those racer design specs…*the sooner I'm debt free.*

"I might be interested. As long as it doesn't affect my work with Hemi. It's important his physical therapy and testing continues." Playing the role of the doting nurse wasn't hard, because deep down she did want to help Hemi. Though her life and future were equally important. She could assume any part needed to get her goals accomplished.

And getting closer to the current racer or Full Throttle's next driver, Jack, had failed to happen. She'd tried getting Jack a drink, talking with him and even had Hemi introduce them. But Jack, for some weird reason, wanted nothing to do with her. She had a nice set of breasts, an ample juicy ass, curves in the right places and hair with deeper curls than ever. Men, women, hell, everyone loved to wrap her curls around their fingers. Except Jack… *Who is an idiot.*

"Great. I've got Snapper, Drag and the guys over in the back meeting room of the Watering Hole and they'd love to talk details, if you don't mind coming with me."

Gina stood up abruptly, her gait a bit awkward for a split second.

"Lead the way."

They marched together side-by-side down the main stretch in Frog Lick. A ridiculous name for a town, but one the Full Throttle gang had decided not to change after their old leader, Bebe Smith, was arrested for allying herself with Shannon's ex-lover and cohort Kascade.

She'd made some weird choices in her life, but sleeping with that megalomaniac had been one of the ones she regretted a bit more.

Really? Getting into debt with Macintosh is probably worse.

Once inside the Watering Hole, Shannon expected more eyes on her, but everyone kept to themselves. Hemi was nursing a tall mug of brew at a table, his gaze on the mug. The bartender, Gaia, was serving up a swath of shots to a small crowd. Maybe some betting had taken place.

"What's the occasion?"

Gina glanced over her shoulder. "Oh, cheering folks up. The test run didn't go as well as we'd hoped. But now that I've got you in here, maybe that will change."

They walked across the wooden floor. The creak of the boards, the graceful maneuvering around mismatched tables and chairs echoed by the chipping paint across multiple surfaces, even the ceiling, caved in at certain places and patched with jagged cut pieces of metal in others, served as a reminder this gang-town sat on the brink. They made things work, but not everything was fully operational.

They aren't building ships either.

Mars was always good for two things — mining and shipbuilding. Where the other gang-towns across three territories had more than racing going for them, the racers and the drivers were all Full Throttle had left. Mining and building brought in the bulk of the revenue, and this gang-town had lost rights to mining and shipbuilding due to the Smiths' betrayal. They needed something to bring in a big amount of flash. The championship for racing would be the only way to do so. For most gang-towns, a win meant extra for members, and potential sponsors from the Upper planets, fools with flash to toss around.

"What exactly do they want me to help with?" Shannon couldn't help but let the concern seep into her tone. She'd been slowly awakening to how much trouble this town was in, how on the edge they all were.

But Bridget Macintosh doesn't care.

"Follow me," Gina replied, heading down a narrow hallway off to the left of a wooden stage with threadbare maroon curtains. The light dimmed in the hallway. Shannon could hear a few voices, mumbling and grumbling over one another behind a closed door ahead.

There was a 'Keep Out' sign in big red letters. Underneath it was scratched into the wood 'The Management.'

Gina didn't even give a knock, just shoved the door open and motioned Shannon into the room.

She entered and found a space almost the size of the bar with three different tables. Hanging fabrics were draped from the ceiling in alternating patterns. Rugs of different shapes, sizes and colors were all over the floor. The scent of whiskey, not the cheap stuff either, lingered in the air along with woodsmoke. A small fire crackled in a metal square enclosure instead of the standard heating element. She was surprised to see them risking a live fire in a flammable space.

Mars was naturally a little chillier than most, especially at night, but nothing like space. The moon, the ships…freezing cold.

"What's up with the fire?" she asked, giving her attention to the room's participants now. Drag, the leader of Full Throttle, with his sun-blond hair and cybernetic arm, sat surrounded by his appointed commanders—Snapper, lead mechanic and Gina's boyfriend, Rune, the cropper and Drag's younger brother and the last option for driver, Jack. Out of the group, three of them had cybernetic parts. She remembered when they'd volunteered for Kascade's experiment.

Jack was the one who frowned at her as he sat down and propped his metal leg on a chair seat. "Maybe you should worry about why you're here."

She scowled at Jack's dismissive tone. Like she was a piece of unwanted dirt or rotted meat. She'd been treated that way once, by the very people she'd thought of as family.

Never again.

"Tell you what, Gina. How about I leave you to your meeting and we can catch up when you decide if my help is really what you need?" She started to pivot on her heel, fully prepared to walk away.

But Drag spoke before she could take another step. "Wait, we require you here. Your expertise would be appreciated. Just ignore Jack. He had a moment today."

"We all have moments. Jack has an attitude… toward me." Shannon squared her shoulders and crossed her arms as she faced the group once more.

"Care to have a seat?" Drag pulled a chair out for her.

Snapper shrugged and spoke at the same time. "Jack's not a fan of outsiders. None of us are."

Shannon took the seat and crossed her legs at her ankles, leaning back and trying to give her best impression of a person who didn't give a shit. Though she needed whatever opportunity they were going to offer her. "I don't care who likes me and who doesn't. I have skills and I try to use those to others' benefits."

Rune smiled at her as he brushed strands of his brown hair out of his eyes. "I knew I liked you for a reason. My brother would like you to use those skills once more to assist us."

"What's the play?" They were beating around a metaphorical bush and Shannon hated it when people didn't talk plainly. Even if half the words were lies, better to spit them out.

Drag laid a hand on Rune's, a signal he'd take over. "Jack is our best driver to replace Hemi. I'm not sure how familiar you are with the rules of the racing commission here on Mars, but in order to replace Hemi as the primary driver, Jack must win the next regional race before the championship. If he doesn't, the expectation is that Hemi will race or there will be no entry for Full Throttle."

"And…Jack looks healthy enough." Shannon glanced over at him, the grumpy asshole with his barely there blond scruff and short blond hair, with tan flesh. Too many days spent out in the sun.

"His cybernetics are causing some difficulties."

Jack, whose brooding gaze, coupled with his eyebrows, had become more pointed by the second, exploded, waving his arms in the air and slamming the cybernetic leg of his onto the chair. The wooden seat split with a crack. "Just fucking say it. I'm defective. My body is rejecting the leg implant and it's starting to malfunction… Fuck, it went into full meltdown on the racetrack. Now the commission's doctor says if I don't get it fixed, I'm not approved to race. But it's worse than a simple leg issue... My nanites are being rejected."

Everyone in the room seemed to freeze, as if Jack's sudden anger weren't normal, but Shannon got it.

"You feel powerless. I understand how that can tear you apart and I can help."

Gazes bored into her, like the drills Mars miners used to carve out Marsanium ore from the caves. This was her chance to play her winning hand, make a demand for her services. But deep down she didn't like Bridget Macintosh or her threats to kill Shannon because she could operate a dice scam better than Mars gang members. Plus, Bridget didn't seem too trustworthy. *Better to pay off the debt my way.* And this was how she'd get there.

Shannon took a deep breath and sat up straight, uncrossing her arms and legs before she rested her elbows against her knees. "I can get you ready to race, but it's going to cost you."

Chapter Three

"Are you fucking joking?" Jack should have been apologizing for the chair. Instead, he focused on squaring off with this cybernetics expert nurse who'd plagued him for longer than she'd ever been in their town. He remembered her—she haunted his dreams and his nightmares as she'd been front and center when he'd undergone the cybernetic procedure to begin with.

Her soothing voice, gorgeous eyes and curly brown hair were imprinted on his psyche and he hated it. Because her being here, when she had the intelligence to work on the Uppers, raised all the red flags. Even as his body, and otherwise prone to flirt and fuck persona, wanted to dismiss them. Women like her didn't get lost on Mars unless they had a reason to hide. But she'd helped save Hemi... *Could maybe save me.*

"When it comes to flash, I don't joke. I also don't make light of my abilities." She leaned up, removing her weight from her chair and scooting it closer to him.

He rolled his eyes at her bragging. She possessed an arrogance he didn't remember from before, and he refused to let a seed of admiration at her confidence take root.

She stood less than a foot from his piece of shit leg. He caught a whiff of musk and lavender. Lavender, like the damn soap Rune's wife Petal created. Her dark-brown luscious curls bounced as she took a seat again. "Your leg's not responding to commands, you're straining. Soon your muscles and energy are going to drain further trying to get it to work. It's going to cause fever. Eventually, brain delirium, and it will spread. Initial tests as we were finalizing the implants had similar results."

He frowned. "You and that psycho you worked for never thought to fix this back then?"

The little shrug she gave as she crossed his arms had his hands aching to throw the broken chair at her. Kascade, her old boss, the one who'd promised him a new future. *Promised all my brothers... We shouldn't have done this to Hemi.*

"Jack's right," Snapper said, clearing his throat. "Why didn't you fix this before?"

"We didn't need to, but I know someone who's worked on the concept since then. Perfecting it."

Bullshit. "I don't believe you."

"Well, it doesn't matter unless your fearless leader wants to scrounge up the flash." She pointed toward Drag.

Drag stroked his chin. Snapper and Gina whispered between each other. Rune kept his eyes on his older brother.

Jack couldn't stand this debate...them deciding how much more of Full Throttle's flash reserves to use to save him. No, he could fight this his own way. Prove his worth. "Tell her to screw off, Drag. I'll find another way or we'll let Hemi heal up and do what we know he can. Sharon here—"

"Shannon."

"Yeah, Susan. She can focus on the real winner." He knew her damn name, but for some reason loved calling her something else, just to see her grind her jaw.

"I think his plan has merit. I'm good to let this spacehole bite the dust."

Good—if she didn't like him, then he could focus on not liking her. Because his body saw the perfect female form and was desperate to get closer, even though this outsider had a true dust honey nature...only looking out for herself.

Gina untangled herself from Snapper's arms and pointed at the door. "How about Shannon and I step out while you four come to a final decision on the matter?"

Shannon stood and scowled at him. "Great idea, and you boys can figure out if Jack's life is worth the flash you'd give up."

Fuck her. Jack almost flipped her the finger but controlled himself even as his gaze drifted to her perfectly shaped ass as she sashayed away. There was plenty for two handfuls and he clenched his hands into fists to fight back the urge. It'd been too long since he'd let himself get buried inside a woman. Exactly why he found the evil nurse so attractive.

If he didn't distrust her true motives so much, he could have appreciated her fine figure a little more. Might even have been willing to see if she'd give him a chance to go for a ride, but... *Women who have tech abilities don't scrounge out a life on Mars.*

Shannon left first, and Gina turned as she was halfway out of the door. "Think about things, but, honestly...she's your best shot."

"Gina's right," added Snapper.

Jack sighed. "You say that because she's your woman and can probably hear every damn word you say. So it's required."

Drag sighed and sat down in the seat Shannon had occupied. "You're being a real ass, Jack."

"Well, I've earned the right. When your body starts breaking down on you, feel free to act like a real turd pounder."

Rune was the next one to slide his seat closer to Jack. "I get you're hurting. Drag acted similarly when he lost his arm and lost Bridget."

"We don't talk about her." Drag slammed his cybernetic arm down on the table, adding a crack to the table to match the chair.

Jack smirked. "At least I'm not riled up by a woman."

"Aren't you?" Snapper parried.

Jack would never admit it, not to this group. He wanted to wallow in his feelings, fall into despair. *You want to act like her.*

"Listen, all of this banter and bullshit is skipping over the point." Drag motioned toward the broken chair and the cracked table. "That's the future for all of us and we're barreling straight for it like a racer headed for the finish line. You want to argue for Hemi to continue on, but he might not be ready in time for the championship. We have to prepare for that possible future. Lay on the other bad news, Snap."

Snapper snapped his cybernetic thumb with his index and middle finger, sending a spark in the air. "We only have one more chance to replace Hemi and two more regional races left to do so. After that, we're locked in."

Rune stamped out the spark before it could catch the table on fire. "This isn't just about the win, though. It's about finding a cure for you that will help my brother, Snapper and Hemi. Because what's happening to you will eventually happen to them."

Way to pile on the guilt. Rune was good at pulling emotions from people when they wanted to hide them. He possessed an uncanny knack for saying the perfect words to make a person think twice.

"I'd rather stay stuck in my pity party of one, please." Jack always sacrificed for the good of the gang and his brothers. These men in this room, and Hemi, had all supported him even as he stood as a reminder of the Smith gang, the past. They treated him like his word and opinions mattered, more so than his own family had.

"Even if this wasn't about the race, you know we'd never let you fall apart. You don't get to die on us yet, Smith or not." Rune reached out and gave him a fake punch to the arm. "We'd be angling for a solve to this no matter what."

"Yeah." Snapper walked around the table. "So, are you going to let our little guilt-tripping, emotionally encouraging discussion go to waste, or do we pay the woman you want to fuck some extra money to get you a cure?"

"Let's hope she doesn't try to scam us into believing the solution is in her pants." Jack couldn't help the crass remark. "And I don't want to fuck her."

"He who protests is usually —"

"Full of shit." Drag slapped his knee with a human hand. "Then it's settled. We'll pay Shannon the flash, if…and that's a big if, she can produce a solution. I'm not giving that amount of crinkle without some results first."

Snapper chuckled. "Thank goodness we have a leader with some brains. Remember when…"

Jack stopped paying attention to the recall. The memories of the Smith gang or even the Macintosh group didn't matter any longer. The past stayed where it was. Besides, all the past held for him were bad memories and lost chances.

The mere mention of the Smiths sent him spiraling mentally to the days when he'd been struggling to find his own identity since the loss of his mother, so soon after his father. All he knew was that he still searched, waiting and wanting his other half…the one his father had always talked about. Though he'd prayed silently for years she would be the one to lift him up. Like Gina did for Snapper… Now with his leg and body failing him, he'd never find her.

Probably die first.

"Enough!" Drag's announcement had Jack sitting up straight in the chair. "Are you good then, Jack? We do this?"

He gave a nod. *If there's a chance…* "I'm in. For the sake of Full Throttle."

Chapter Four

"Why do you dislike Jack so much?"

Gina posed the question to Shannon once they were out of the hallway and in the main room of the Watering Hole.

"I think I need a drink before I start sharing things with you like we're best friends." Shannon didn't bother glancing back, just headed straight for the bar.

Both Hemi and the crowd were no longer there. They'd moved off and gathered at tables near the stage where some older gentleman—a semi-regular fixture from what Shannon had seen—had set up with his guitar. Hemi sat there, front and center, drinking as the guitar player strummed a long wail of a ballad.

Shannon reached the bar, slid onto one of the wooden stools and bumped her fist against the bar top twice.

"Be right there," Gaia said, swiveling on her feet with the grace of a dancer, her twin blonde braids waving in the air as she moved back and forth assembling food and drinks.

Shannon tapped her toe against the leg of the stool, anxious to hear what Drag and the others decided, nervous if she'd played her hand too hard. She needed an opening... Her time was running out. When the opportunity to play nurse for Hemi came up, that was when Bridget had given her the opportunity in place of coming up with the flash outright. But the Macintosh leader had given her only a six-week window. Six weeks ended today.

Shannon had kept her focus on Hemi, because anything else seemed to only get her side-eyes from others. Not to mention, outside of her patient, Gina was the only one who would really talk to her, not Snapper or Drag. The others in the bar and in town were friendly, but like any gang, unwilling to open up to outsiders unless their leader gave the word.

Her reputation and past with the cyborgs here had gotten her into the town itself, even earned her a place to rest her head, food and drink without the expectation of pay, but otherwise they treated her like an off-worlder. Not worthy enough to court favor with like so many did for those visiting from the Uppers, who had the flash to raise a gang out of the ashes.

No, I'll never be good enough for that.

"Are there certain topics only limited to best friends?" Gina saddled up on the stool next to Shannon.

"Huh?" She'd gotten distracted by her bitterness.

"You mentioned sharing things with a friend. Are there topics you only save for them?"

"Yeah, there are some. I don't go around telling everything about me to everyone."

Gina adjusted herself and angled to face Shannon. "Makes sense. Can you tell me about Hemi, though? Do you think…if Jack says no, that is, will Hemi be ready to race within the next two months?"

"I honestly don't know." Talking about him had Shannon glancing over her shoulder at the man himself.

Hemi was positioned fairly close to the stage, non-cybernetic hand holding his mug high and waving slowly back and forth in the air to the latest song playing. "His confidence was shattered from the accident. He's mentioned having nightmares and adjusting to cybernetics is challenging for those replacing a single limb… Half a body is unheard of." She'd marveled at the concept of a person made of equal parts machine and human because Shannon had thought it impossible until she'd been asked to come to Frog Lick.

Gaia came over to them, placing her palms flush against the wood. Her expression was all business—flat lips, no smile to her eyes. Another person who barely tolerated Shannon. "What can I get you?"

"A brew, whatever you want to pour." Shannon always said the same thing—doing her best to try to win the woman over because she'd be a good insight into others, but like Gina, the bartender refused to give her a chance outside of providing food and drink.

"Gina?"

"Same as what Shannon's having."

The bartender smiled then. "You know I serve her the bottom of the barrel brew. That weakling ale no one likes."

Gina's face contorted in disgust. "Why? This woman's a hired guest of Full Throttle. She's taking good care of Hemi and you're treating her like she's some enemy."

Those words made Shannon sit up a bit straighter. Maybe Gina wasn't like everyone else after all. Shannon's foolish heart clenched a bit and she thumped her chest twice with a flick of her thumb to clear the useless desire for friendship and closeness away. Tender emotions weren't for her, not after what she'd done and even more what she was willing to do.

Gaia's smile faded, her gaze a bit sheepish. "I apologize. I'll get you both the house special."

The bartender walked away and Shannon bit her lip to keep from commenting on the set-down Gina had given the woman.

"People don't mean to be so cruel. I promise. It's often they don't know any better. This world seems to breed a natural distrust."

Don't I know it.

"It's all right." It wasn't, but Shannon had forced herself to stop caring long ago. "I won't be around long enough to worry about making connections."

"But you see the purpose of getting Jack fixed? You understand the predicament we're in and survival…"

Mugs clicked against each other as Gaia set them down, foaming spilling over the sides. "On the house, for my previous attitude. We do appreciate Hemi getting the help he needs. He's one of the good ones. Hell, all the racers and mechanics are."

Shannon picked up the mug and took a quick sip. "We're all good until someone gives us a reason not to be."

Gaia raised a single blonde eyebrow in response and Shannon winked. She liked to keep people guessing. Those who underestimated her did so at their peril.

"We'll let you know if we need anything, Gaia." Gina grabbed her mug, oblivious to the exchange.

Shannon didn't miss some sort of unspoken communication between the two, though. But she'd let them have their private moment. Everyone in this town had a bunch of those and she'd lost her curiosity for such things when her gang-town had sold her off to the moonies.

Inter-gang-town politics were a waste of a person's time and patience. Exactly why Shannon enjoyed traveling from town-to-town, finding her own fortune and making her own way. She'd never belonged anywhere before, and the two times she'd tried had only ended in disappointment.

Never forget it.

So, Shannon took a couple more gulps of brew before Gina spoke next.

"Then, if what you're saying about Hemi is true and you know what this means to us, is the flash really worth all that much?"

Funny, Gina was playing the emotional card. The 'if you cared, you'd do this.' How many times had she heard those impassioned speeches over the past couple decades of her life? "*Sacrifice yourself for the greater good.*"

Those words had been used by her father, her adoptive parents and even Kascade, though never once had giving provided her anything in return. No, she made deals, but they cost something. Because everything had a price.

"Is paying for someone's connections and ability not worth it? The conversation can work both ways. The bottom line, I don't give things away for free. You wouldn't give stuff away either and don't mention the drink."

Gina turned her mug, the handle moving back and forth between her hands. "Your reasoning has logic, but I had to try."

"Well, let me point out if Drag doesn't agree to pay or Jack refuses to cooperate, these problems aren't going to go away. I was there when they all had the cybernetics implanted. There were risks then and there is a reason that until Hemi, and whatever trick you used to get the cybernetic doctor out of retirement, there were only three cybernetic test subjects.

"What we attempted was risky. Now Hemi is going to run into the same problems as the others. Maybe worse ones due to the amount of cybernetics you gave him. Is it really saving his life, if he ends up suffering worse than if you'd let him die?"

There were plenty of emotional triggers she could push, too.

"You gave my friend Sampson the doctor's information and we're grateful. He believed in using the technology to save Hemi's life and I guess I hoped you might believe in prolonging these men's as well."

Shannon chuckled and ran a finger along the rope chain at her neck, trailing back and forth. "No one does things out of the goodness of their heart, and I won't be the sucker to start. It's not polite to play those offering their skills and services."

Gina sighed. "We are grateful for what you've done so far."

"Well, supposedly she can do more...for a price." Jack's voice rang out crystal clear as he leaned on the bar next to her, then yanked her mug out of her hands. He downed the rest of her drink.

"The hell?"

"That's exactly what we're going to be in for however long it will take for you to deliver on your promises." He slammed the mug on the bar top. "That's good shit. Gaia, Shannon needs a refill."

She twisted in her seat facing Jack, lifting her necklace out from under her shirt to grab a hold of the white indented bone charm there, her special talisman. "Then Drag has agreed."

"First payment he'll bring out to you right here. So don't go anywhere. Make your plans, but we head out to meet your contact within the next two days."

Two days wasn't enough. She needed to contact Bridget, make arrangements and set up Hemi's physical therapy plan before she headed out. No sense in risking flash.

"I'm gonna need more time than that."

"Well, two days is all you're going to get." Jack winked at her and walked off. His gait was slowed, but he still possessed plenty of strength and looking at his ass wasn't a hardship either.

Well, damn.

Chapter Five

Shannon sat in the cold metal room where she worked with Hemi and waited. She didn't want to risk drawing attention to her presence from other folks wandering the street, so she sat in the dark. The only illumination was from the rays of Mars' larger moon, Phobos, shining through a broken window.

There was a light breeze in the air, bringing with it the scent of burning wood and a sharp metallic bite — iron and Marsanium being processed.

They may not be able to build ships, but they're still stockpiling.

A long howl and the rattle of metal containers clanging against each other somewhere outside made her jump.

"Fuck," she muttered under her breath. She'd left her signal for Bridget's spies and she was almost out of time.

They were set to leave in the morning and so far her newfound agreement with Full Throttle had yielded no results. She'd spent the better part of the day prepping Hemi's physical therapy plan in her absence, sending a holo-communication to her friend on the nanites and wishing she could have found a way to steal the plans.

She still couldn't go into the mechanics bay. She'd hoped signing up to help Jack would give her a little more access to other areas of Frog Lick, but no such thing. Her attempts to enter had been thwarted three different times. Any excuse was dismissed as nothing urgent and she was told to go to the Watering Hole after hours if she wanted to speak to anyone.

"You make a lot of noise."

She jumped again and this time almost fell out of the seat. "Double fuck. You think you could not sneak up on people?"

The chuckle that echoed around the room, a low sound she couldn't identify as male or female, had her skin breaking out with chill bumps.

"I get paid to be sneaky. You left a message and Bridget wants to know if you have the designs." Stepping out of the dark shadows in the corner of the room, one of Bridget's spies came into view. They were covered head to toe in dark fabric, wrapped up like some sort of monster from ancient Earth stories. Their eyes glowed faintly, a reminder they were enhanced. Several assassins had found moonie doctors willing to try experimental surgeries with less concern about the safety of the humans they operated on.

"You can see in the dark, but what other tricks did they give you?" She sat up straight in her chair and crossed her legs and arms. *Show strength, not fear.*

"It doesn't matter what enhancements I possess. Answer the question or I add pain to the situation."

They spoke dispassionately as if the end goal didn't matter.

Shannon took a minute to analyze this spy, most likely a hired assassin. They weren't much bigger than her. She could try to make a run for it if needed, let out a scream. "I don't have the designs. It's near impossible to gain access to them. The mechanics bay is locked down tight enough even you can't infiltrate it."

The glow in their eyes increased, damn near predatory. "The point isn't if I could... This is your bargain. You didn't meet it, so you die."

They started to approach and for a split second Shannon froze. The fear slid through her veins, as if infusing to her bones. Imminent death. *No one kills me, I choose my fate.*

She leaned over and grabbed the bag at her feet with one hand, while she gripped the talisman she wore around her neck with the other. She tossed the bag toward the approaching assassin and it hit them in the stomach.

They stopped as the bag fell to the floor at their feet, having no impact other than to get a glance from them. "That's the best defense you have? It's not a bomb."

"It's flash. A portion of the debt I owe. Take that to Bridget and let her know I'll have what she needs within two weeks. Just two more weeks." Time was all she wanted.

"This doesn't change the payment promised."

"I'm aware." She'd figured it wouldn't, even though a nicer person might have been willing to negotiate. There was a lot of crinkle in the bag, enough to get Shannon close to buying a small lot on a Jupiter moon. She could've run.

The assassin spy picked up the bag. "I'll relay your request, but if she doesn't accept, expect my return."

Shannon nodded. "Fine, whatever. I'll keep working in the meantime."

They gave no additional response, just stepped into the shadows and disappeared from sight.

Shannon didn't recall a hole in the wall there or even a tunnel, but she was far too concerned with her survival to bother finding out. She stood and kept her focus on that corner as she made to exit the building. Once outside, she strolled toward the Watering Hole. She'd stay there until close.

* * * *

The next morning, she arrived at the mechanics bay doors just as the starting bell chimed, signaling the beginning of the workday for the miners, mechanics, brewers, horticulturists, airponics workers and more. The town of Frog Lick became a veritable cornucopia of folks heading to and fro with smiles, friendly greetings and playful banter… *It's strange.*

Hell, they even had a school for the kids. Her gang-town, Zephyr, believed children needed to occupy themselves while the adults worked. Forget reading and writing—any education at all was forged by watching, and since most folks didn't care, those in Zephyr ended up not amounting to much unless they fought for what they wanted. *Or got sold off.*

There were times she didn't regret escaping this hell-hole of a planet. Though maybe if more places were like Frog Lick, it wouldn't be so damn awful. *Stop thinking fantasies.*

"What the hell are you doing here?" Jack's aggravated tone helped wash away her fruitless musings.

She glanced over at him and tried not to be attracted to those deep blue eyes that looked at her with dislike. She was the one trying to help him. *Spacehole.*

"You said we leave today. Just trying to figure out the plan."

"I was going to come by this afternoon. Have some stuff I need to wrap up, then pack the vehicle with supplies—"

"We're taking the racer?" Maybe her luck might finally change.

Jack snorted. "You'd like that, wouldn't you? Been angling for a look at that damn thing ever since you showed up. No, we're taking a hauler. As soon as the bell rings for the day, we'll depart."

She relaxed against the metal wall of the building, soaking up the warmth already gathering from the rising sun, then she adjusted the sun goggles over her eyes. "Why is it when I've only ever tried to help you and your friends, you always think the worst of me?"

"My father always said if it talks shit, it probably is—"

The double doors to the mechanics bay burst open and Snapper stepped outside. "Jack, the hell? We need you right now. I need extra torque and...oh, sorry, didn't know you were in the middle of something. Hello, Shannon. Hope you're having a good morning."

Shannon gave Snapper a nod. "It's good to know one of you cyborgs has manners. Might do your friend Jack a favor and teach him how to be polite to people. Especially the person who's going to risk her neck to save his life."

Jack gave a half-chuckle, half-snort. "You're acting like you're doing this because you care, but you're getting paid for it. Quit pretending. When you stop with the fake sentiment and want-to-be-friends routine, maybe I'll bother being polite to you."

"You must have been seriously tricked as a child to be so mistrusting. Did momma or poppa not feed you enough? Maybe they didn't spend any time with you?"

The scowl on Jack's face turned downright predatory...something she'd only seen on people with a mind to murder.

He opened his mouth to say something then immediately closed it, stomping off past Snapper and into the bay.

Snapper let out a low whistle. "Damn, I mean...he's the one we consider nice. The lady charmer. For you to piss him off so bad he looks ready to strangle something, my people and my woman are not going to be thanking you today."

"Just tell him I'll be ready to go at the bell, and I'll be at the shack you call a doctor's facility." She decided to walk off then, adjusting her goggles against the sun's rays. The accusations Jack hurled her way weren't lies, but it damn well pissed her off. Especially when she had problems just like he did, and she was doing her best to solve them.

Only no one will let me.

* * * *

"You really hate that woman. Why?" Snapper asked, marching up next to Jack.

Bent over, wrench in hand and loosening a bolt, Jack debated on responding because the truth would be childish and ridiculous. The other option made him sound more like Snapper than he ever cared to be.

Snapper tapped the bumper with his cybernetic arm. "Not leaving until you give me something because I don't like the idea of putting you two in a hauler heading on a cross-country mission of mercy. She knows how your cybernetics work and she could kill you."

Jack chuckled, at first in a self-deprecating way then with a little more conviction. Of course, the woman who wore the necklace he'd made for his mother a long time ago would be the very person who was supposed to save his life. Irony at its finest. The god, goddess…whatever fucking deity created this hellscape had come back to deliver agony on him in multiple ways

And I only ever did good things.

Or at least Jack thought he had. "Think of it this way." He moved out from underneath the hood and stood up straight, the wrench in one hand and the loosened bolt in the other. "If she kills me, you and Drag won't have to pay her."

"Yeah, but then it's a revenge mission. You're our brother."

"Not by blood." Compared to the rest of the leaders of Full Throttle, he was the outsider. The leftover from the previous gang who stuck around because where the hell else did he have to go? Frog Lick was his home, the mechanics bay his second skin, the refuge when a woman's arms didn't cut it.

"You're family regardless." Snapper smacked on his metal arm. "This, your leg, the nanites running through our blood connect us together. We went through an ordeal, a transformation, and lived. So, stuff those impostor thoughts back in the hole they emerged from and tell me what the hell about this woman is driving you nuts?"

Jack opened his mouth then closed it. What the hell did he say?

"For the first time he's attracted to someone and doesn't know how to act?" Hemi stepped up then.

"I'm not—"

"Don't even lie. I've watched you give her more than a few visual appraisals."

Jack shook his head. "Yeah, but I was going to say I'm not going to intrude on another brother's territory. Or fuck with a potential business arrangement."

That was the reputation he'd built. The ladies liked him, they entertained him and he kept a select clientele happy until they found something permanent. But he wasn't in the market for something built to last long term. At least that was the lie he sold them on.

Because you were waiting for the necklace. Fuck.

"Another brother?"

"He means me." The announcement came with the slide and grind of Hemi's too heavy walk, his inability to perfectly balance himself with his cybernetic half and human side. Add in the click of the cane he used and Jack could have sworn Hemi might be able to create his own music.

Snapper cocked his head to the side. "You got the hots for your nurse, Hemi?"

"If I do, the feelings are not mutual."

Snapper laughed as he glanced between the two of them. "You both are ridiculous. Jack, finish up whatever you're tweaking on that hauler. Then meet up with me and Drag in the office, before the finish bell. We should go over some details."

Jack gave a single nod and watched Snapper walk off, shaking his head. Hemi kept moving until he stood beside Jack.

"So, traveling to Auster…with Shannon."

He'd barely slept contemplating the sheer insanity. Auster…hell, Jack had never ventured outside Wespero except the one time he'd had to race in the main dome in Aurora territory. Even then, he'd traveled with a crew from Frog Lick.

"Yeah, seems like the dumbest idea I've had yet. How about you go instead?"

Hemi shook his head. "I'm damaged goods. Can still barely walk. Sure, you're not peak health, but you can handle yourself a bit better than I would be able to."

Jack shrugged. "Maybe. But don't dismiss yourself. You're learning and the adjustment takes time."

"Yeah…sure. Is it true though? The nanites are degrading?"

Jack glanced around, looking for interested glances. Sure, everyone in the bay had been vetted, but gossip in this small town only fueled concerns for the coming races. Everyone was already feeling nervous with losing Full Throttle's shipbuilding permits and the inability to sell Marsanium. They were starting to fill up spaceship hangers with the stuff.

"It's only affecting me. Let's leave it at that. Shannon happens to know someone who might be able to fix the issue, but everyone else is fine."

The deep sighs coming from his friend were bothersome. "All right, I'll leave it lie. Just…treat her good, not like those other women you're always hanging around."

"Hemi…I am not interested in that way." Not exactly true, but physicality and desire needed to be put to a halt. Even if the necklace around her neck meant otherwise to him.

"Denial is a hard beast to beat, but I'll say this—I like her, and I want her to come back. She doesn't put up with my bullshit and has helped me a lot. Her skills with this cybernetic crap are no lie."

Jack waved him off. "Nothing to worry about here. Let me fix this damn hauler so we can make sure to leave after the quitting bell. The sooner we're gone, the sooner we're back."

And he'd get some damn peace and quiet for a few hours. He didn't want to talk about Shannon anymore. Not about her knowledge, her likability or her looks. The fucking way she acted all tough, even when she didn't have the upper hand. Her snarky retorts, that curly dark brown hair he wanted to plunge his fucking hands into and grab hold of.

Jack shook his head with a growl and Hemi laughed. "All right. Looks like you'll punish yourself more than I ever will. Later."

The work on the hauler went a little smoother after Jack got some alone time, though his body seemed intent on penalizing him, from dropped wrenches, to miscalculating the distance between his head and the engine cover. An hour or so before the final bell, he'd managed to get the hauler tuned up, extra fuel in canisters and supplies assembled.

His mood hadn't improved. Leaving Frog Lick with barely four weeks before the next race bothered him. There were obligations he needed to meet. *And you need a functioning body to meet them.*

Jack squeezed his fists together and took a deep breath. He'd have to let go of this animosity toward Shannon and pray she could deliver on her promises.

Because already his worst fears were starting to come true — becoming of a shell of himself...like his father.

Nope, not ending up like him.

"Hey, Jack...are you wrapped up? Drag wanted a minute." Gina poked her head around the hauler. She stepped out, spreading her hands out over the hauler's side panel as she looked at the engine. "This looks good. You cleaned it up?"

"Yeah, no sense in traveling across Mars looking like another hunk of junk." The truth was he'd gotten lost in menial tasks, letting his mind wander. Debating the possibilities of the future, of what could go wrong on the road with Shannon and thinking a few scenarios he needed to shake away versus embrace. That damn necklace Shannon wore fueled those musings. *Wish I'd never noticed it.*

"Well, I wouldn't want you to draw attention to yourself."

He shrugged. "Doubtful. This hunk of metal will be covered in dust within the first couple hours. Tell Drag I'm coming."

Instead of turning and leaving, she approached him, closing the gap. He noticed her movements were hesitant as if she couldn't understand how he might react.

"Everything okay?"

"I just don't like you traveling alone, without one of us." She reached and laid a hand on his shoulder. "Come back safe and make good decisions because without you...well, I don't want to think about Full Throttle without Jack. And it's only one month until the next race."

He chuckled a little bit. This outward display of affection from Gina was a little weird, especially when she saved all of her emotional output for Snapper. "If I didn't know better, I might think you had a crush on me, Gina."

"A crush? Is that the same concept as smothering something?"

The small laugh he had turned into a big one. "No, but an interesting comparison. I'll make sure I come back. That's a promise."

Gina frowned. "Then you better keep it."

Chapter Six

Jack tapped on the door to Snapper's office before entering. The door itself was open, with Snapper and Drag inside. They were seated, sharing cups of amber liquid and chatting as if they didn't have a care in the world.

The grins on their faces, the casual relaxation in their frames...This shit he would miss. *Quit thinking like you're already dead.*

The friendships he'd made, though limited, had helped buoy him in a place where he'd felt alone for years. The cybernetic connection they all had gave him a bond to people in ways that meant more than blood.

They shared limitations, fears and plenty of strengths. Without those common things —

"You just going to stand in the door, or do you want a drink?" Snapper asked and Drag glanced over his shoulder at him.

No more sulking in the doorway.

"I'll pass on the drink. Want to be fully alert for the trip."

Drag nodded his agreement. "Good call. I already like how you're thinking about this and wanted to talk to you about Shannon and going into Auster."

"What about it?" Jack moved further into the room, toward Snapper's bookshelves along the wall. There was an extra chair, but he'd be sitting enough the next week. Standing made him feel stronger, allowed him to push back the doubts and fears his leg would give out at any moment.

"Be prepared for anything. She says she has someone who can help, but help doesn't come for free. Watch for the double cross and, if you feel it's necessary, ditch her once she gets you access to the tech we need. We can pay her when she makes her way back here. Gina is capable of figuring out the rest."

Jack bunched his eyebrows, disliking the uncomfortable sensation gathering in his chest at the idea of Shannon hurt. "Gina would kill Shannon?"

Snapper blew out a sharp burst of air, then laughed. "No, she can take care of inputting the tech. Gina's not hurting anyone."

Relief flooded him, releasing some tension held in his sternum, stress that had coiled tight at Drag's words. Already, the necklace, the memories, the silent promises he'd made based on the stories his father had shared — Jack had pinned his future on a piece of jewelry and knowing it was back seemed to affect all his intentions. *Shit.*

Jack faced toward the shelves, fingering the spines of the books there. Old engine manuals, assembly pages and tales of different types of engines.

"Can you do that, Jack? Put yourself first?" Drag took a sip and when Jack found himself unable to speak right away, Drag continued. "You said it yourself — we can't trust her. Nothing's changed, correct?"

"Not if you saw the way he acted toward her this morning," Snapper volunteered.

Had it really been only half a day, no more than a few hours? Jack's animosity had faded with each fantasy he let play out in his mind. *Idiot.*

He turned sharply and a twinge of pain shot up his cybernetic leg at the quick movement. "I'll do what I must. If she doesn't deliver or if she does but shows signs of betrayal, I'll get out of there. No way am I going to jeopardize Full Throttle. Not with Hemi's status unknown."

Drag gave him a smile and a nod. "Exactly what I want to hear."

The bell rang, echoing through the town. Work was complete in the mines for the day. The mechanics would shut down as well. People would gather at the Watering Hole and Jack... He'd be leaving town.

"You're all set?" Snapper asked.

"Yeah, hauler is prepped. Need to swing by my place for some clothes."

Snapper grinned. "Did Gina visit you? She's pretty worried."

Jack would ignore the tightness in his chest, the reminder people cared about him. "Yeah, so did Hemi. Like you are giving me some sort of 'never coming home' send-off. I'm not a kid, but a grown-ass man."

"Humor them," Snapper said, his smile melting away to a somber expression. There a memory there. Hell, they all had them... Jack recalled the last time he'd spoken to his father, before the mining accident.

"I did. And I'll humor you both too. Any words of wisdom or fuzzy feelings?" Jack tried to go for a light-hearted tone.

"Wear protection."

"Don't stick it without permission."

Snapper and Drag spoke at the same time, then all three of them broke out into laughter. The words were a joke they'd shared countless times about racing and fucking.

"The best advice to live by."

* * * *

The hauler pulled up in front of her makeshift work building exactly thirty minutes after the closing bell. She'd been ready, a bag slung over her shoulder with everything she owned.

"Travel light." Those were words to live by and ones she did, ever since she'd lost everything leaving Mars for a life on the Earth's moon. The fact she didn't stick in one place very long or that her adoptive parents preferred to move around the various moonie bases to keep things 'fresh for their minds' made Shannon appreciate having a small amount of personal possessions.

As long as she had clothes on her back, boots on her feet and her necklace, everything would work out.

A weapon on person is nice, too.

But she could make weapons. Her knowledge of the human body meant she could as easily poison someone as fast as she helped them.

"Wow." She smiled at the squeaky-clean hauler stopped in front of her. The metal gleam of the hood, the shine on the glass…even the wheels looked brand-new. "You got this baby all dressed up for me?"

Jack rolled his eyes and put the hauler in park. "Afraid it's more a precaution and to ensure no damage than to impress you."

Of course, he didn't like her, but she had to keep trying. The clock was still ticking and she was pissed at the flash she'd already tossed away without anything to show for her sacrifice. Her life was still on the line. One way or another, after this trip, she'd change how things played out.

She tossed her bag in the backseat and it clunked. "Did you have to pack your whole house?"

"I thought women liked a guy with plenty of luggage?"

She snorted indelicately and didn't give a damn. "We meant what you've got in your pants. Where I come from, you learn to pack light. Never know when you'll need to be on the move, or the next opportunity is going to strike."

"You mean, not knowing when the law is coming after you?"

Shannon let out a mocking gasp as she stood there on the other side of the hauler door. "Are you honestly accusing me of being a criminal?"

"If the shoe fits… You did associate with Kascade, leader of Humans First, a terrorist organization."

A big mistake. One she'd come to peace with a long time ago. It served as a reminder not to let stars get in her eyes. People she tended to care for often didn't give two shits about her. "And, if I remember correctly, you and your brothers associated with us as well?"

He mulled that one, grinding his jaw as he looked at her. "Fair enough. Hop in and let's get a move on."

Shannon refused to hop. She opened the door, listening for the tell-tale creak found on vehicles made from heavily cut and re-used metal. Instead, it was smooth sailing. Sliding into the seat, she shut the door behind her then looked for the safety strap. "Do you supply protection in these vehicles?"

One eyebrow raised, Jack glanced at her lap then slowly dragged his gaze upward. Her skin heated at his perusal. Suddenly she started to second-guess the idea he didn't like her. Maybe he disliked being attracted to her?

Even better.

"You're sitting on it." He glanced away then, taking stock of the gauges and measurement on the dash, while she dug her hands under her ass.

Sure enough, she pulled out two straps with a metal buckle at one end.

"How fast does this go?" she asked as she secured the strap and tightened it down to keep her locked in the seat.

"Fast enough you'll want to stay locked in. Also, once we clear the main roads it can get a little bumpy so I hope you emptied your bladder because we're not stopping until we're halfway to the territory marker."

* * * *

As the sun set and Shannon took her sun goggles off, they kept silent. The ride did get bumpy as the main clear paths through Wespero gave way to the less traveled areas where Jack had to get a little more creative with his driving, avoiding plants, rocks, and in some cases, animals.

She took the silence as a chance to reflect and confront her fears of the person who'd threatened her last night. She'd met Bridget's would-be assassin only once before and hadn't been intimidated. *Not until I saw those damn eyes.*

Her brain chose that moment to recall Hemi's kind-hearted plea for Shannon to be safe. She'd almost laughed at him because she'd never played things cautious and wouldn't start any time soon. But the man's amber gaze and his concerned bearing made her give him reassurances even if she couldn't keep them.

Her focus needed to be on her future. How would she get access to the plans? Jack's little reveal with his eyes told her there were still areas she could exploit. Now that she'd be in close proximity to him, maybe it was worth trying to build his attraction to her.

Funny. She'd always thought him the best looking out of the other Full Throttle cyborgs. He had dirty blond hair, kept short and cropped, and a myriad of tattoos on his arms she found interesting. There were phrases in other languages, images of moons and suns…and a symbol, the same one on her necklace.

Maybe her necklace meant something else. She was tempted to ask him about it. Instead, she kept silent and pondered how getting Jack to engage with her sexually would get her anywhere near those plans. She'd have to break into the damn mechanics bay. Lull him into a stupor, steal the hauler and head back… *No, stupid idea.*

Each potential idea fail only wound her tighter until she was clenching her fists against her thighs. She raised one to her stomach and rubbed against her belly.

"You get motion sick or something?"

"What?" Jack's question threw her for a minute.

Then he pointed at her stomach. "You're acting like you don't feel good. Do I need to drive slower or stop? I'm not a fan of puke and definitely don't want this hauler smelling like vomit for the next week."

She chuckled. "No, I'm good. Got a lot on my mind..."

I need to say something. Fuck, what?

She couldn't go with the present truth but could definitely stick to the past. "Where we're going... Auster. It's not exactly the nicest territory on Mars. I think that award goes to Wespero. The gang-towns there are more—"

"Barbaric. I think we've all heard the tales. People living in mounds of dirt. No buildings, barely any shoes or clothes. Lots of sandstorms." Those words were spoken as if they were rumor. Fairytales, similar to those from Earth. Told with a slight humor in their phrasing, the concept of being too far-fetched to be real.

"Those are exaggerations, but they hold truth. The storms are real though. Horrible things. We definitely were given the worst part of Mars to inhabit."

"We? You grew up in Auster?"

She refused to share stories of a past she'd taken great pains to block out, of memories she'd stuffed down inside her so deep not even a top-notch Mars mining crew could reach them.

"I'm not here to tell you tales of my childhood. I am saying we need to be prepared to take shelter without hesitation, stopping in optimal places that don't leave us in the open. The wildlife isn't too friendly either. There are yoties and coon cats. The worst are the damn slithers."

"Slithers is a damn made-up word. We deal with plenty of those first two in Wespero, though the populations aren't big. I imagine as we get more species here, fur-buns and the like, we're going to see an increase."

She frowned. "Slithers are real as the ground we drive on. They were brought, a case full, to a gang-town leader who wanted to use them to display wealth after their gang-town won Auster its first and only racing championship. Only the leader made a mistake, thought the things were harmless and they escaped their enclave. Ate the whole damn town. Now they roam Auster, underground and coming up periodically."

Jack shivered and gripped the steering wheel tighter. "That's some bullshit story designed to scare kids and keep them from wandering off to places they shouldn't. I'll believe it when I see it."

"You see one of them and you're too late." Shannon recalled the loss of several able-bodied miners due to a slither encounter. She refused to repeat the scenario. "Best way to ward them off is with heat. They don't like heat, which is why they tend to come out more at night."

"And you didn't think to mention this before we took off and the sun went down?"

Shannon bite back a smile. "We're not in Auster territory yet."

"Good news is we'll be fine. I have a heating unit that is solar powered during the day and will last for up to twelve hours on a full charge. Should heat up the tent and the surrounding area nicely."

"You mean tents, plural?"

Jack chuckled, his gaze periodically glancing her way. His laughter became more pronounced with each look. "I'm talking tent, singular. The food and all the other supplies meant we had to economize."

She crossed her arms, not liking how this would force her toward being closer to Jack. *Which is what you want, right?*

She hadn't decided how she wanted this to play out. Seducing him would help her cause, but her body liked the idea too much. Though there was no sense fighting against sharing a tent with a too big, too sexy man who disliked her. Sleeping outside on the hard, cold ground would be unacceptable.

"Anything else I need to know about this foreign territory?"

His question got her mind hurtling toward the deep cave of memories she swore never to let out and she focused on the basic facts—the ones she didn't need her childhood to recall.

"You were right. These gangs are a little more barbaric in the fact they take what they want. Doesn't matter your affiliation—if you get caught on your own, expect trouble. Best to travel through the towns, not stay in them. There are a couple that might be safe.

"Auster and the gangs here have won the least amount of racing championships, as you know, so I wouldn't volunteer where you're from. Best to say traveling from the dome or even say you're coming from Aurora territory. Where we're headed, Wespero folks are the enemy."

Jack scoffed. "And you wanted to bring the racer. What's our first stop after we get to the border?"

"Let's focus on the border for now." She uncrossed her arms and rubbed her palms against her thighs. A thin layer of sweat had gathered on her palms, the curse of her body heat and the cooling night air.

"You cold?" His observation and general interest in her wellbeing wreaked a little havoc on her senses. This was unlike what she'd become familiar with from him. She didn't want to catch any feelings with this one. Not when she had a job her life hinged upon.

She shook her head. "No, fine for now."

Because either way, whether she stoked this attraction between him or he did, Jack was going to hate her by the time she wrapped this whole mess up.

Chapter Seven

Jack had meant to ask about the necklace. It had been on the tip of his tongue to bring it up. Where had she gotten the jewelry? How had it come into her possession?

Instead, he'd seen those clenched fists and found himself worried she'd be ill, concerned with the trip affecting her. He shouldn't have cared, yet there was no lying to himself that since he'd seen the necklace she wore—the necklace he'd created for his mother all those years ago—the urge to protect had emerged something fierce.

The idea they would share one tent, constantly in close proximity to each other, failed to help him focus either, which was why he pushed the hauler farther, driving an extra couple of hours past when he'd planned to stop until they were on the road long past sundown. The moons of Mars were visible and bright overhead.

Eventually he'd have to confront this attraction to Shannon, along with this growing desire to get to know her, all because she wore his jewelry. Dumb idea, but one he'd clung to since he was small, since his father had soothed him to sleep after a day of crying and devastation.

"The necklace will come back to you, and when it does, it will bring someone to share a life with."

Those words were ever present now as the Auster Territory sign appeared in the distance, two bright lights reflecting off the words carved and painted into a large rock.

Jack slowed the hauler to a crawl. "Do we cross into the territory or stay on the Wespero side for the night?"

"Wespero side. I mean, the checkpoint is literally three buildings. The checkpoint, the housing and the bar. We'd be better served to keep people unaware of our presence until tomorrow," Shannon replied. She sat leaned back in her seat, goggles around her neck, gaze upward at the twinkling sky above. "Just camp near the sign, behind the boulder."

He drove the hauler into place and immediately got to work setting up camp. Shannon wasn't much help, but she unloaded a few things and took basic directions for getting their water ready. Then she started to assist with the tent.

Her struggling grunts as she tried to stake a pole into the ground got his attention.

"Need help?"

Shannon huffed a few curls out of her face, her skin flushed from exertion even with the cooler night air. "No, I'll figure it out eventually or choose to sleep in the hauler. Is that an option?"

Jack sided up close to her and bent down to wrap his hand around the mallet she held. "Can I show you?"

She tensed briefly then relaxed as she gave a nod.

He moved in closer, taking in the scent of soap and a flowery healing balm she'd given Hemi to use on his cybernetic parts. Seemed she used the same stuff as well.

They worked together, him showing her how much pressure to put with her strikes and using his leg to fix her stance.

"I thought you were familiar with roughing it, being a nomad on Mars." He felt her stiffen beneath him again. "I don't mean that as an insult, just wondering."

She took control over the next swing, adding more of her weight and Jack let her direct the mallet. "I tend to plan accordingly so I'm never out in the elements by myself."

"Not a fan of camping?" The stake secure, Jack reluctantly moved away from her, immediately disliking the separation.

Shannon walked over to the next stake and proceeded to follow Jack's previous direction perfectly. "I can't say I like the idea. But you haven't lived in Auster. Even underground is better than exposure like this. The heat should work but..." She shrugged. "I don't trust it."

"Well, you won't be alone."

She snapped her head up and looked at him, a surprised glint in her eyes.

He cleared his throat. "I didn't mean...I'm not expecting anything... Shit."

"So much for the infamous Jack Renfrow charm. Could it kill you to pretend to find me attractive?"

"It's got nothing to do with whether I want you or not." He turned on his heel and went back to the hauler to make sure they had everything. *Let those words sink in for a moment.*

This attraction wasn't something he should fool around with, not until he knew her plans. Would she go wandering off again when Hemi was recovered? Hell, he still wasn't even sure why she'd taken the job to begin with, and her fascination with the mechanics bay, the racer…too many odd inquiries to not suspect something more sinister. She reminded him of his mother, looking out for only herself and thinking nothing of others. He needed to cut this interest off before it messed with him even more, necklace be damned.

With the tent secure, Jack started to move the heating element, a heavy box with handles toward the tent entrance. It would stay outside to project heat from the coils within.

"Damn, Shannon. Can you grab that black box in the back of the hauler?"

She dropped the mallet in her hand and walked over to the four-seater. "Which box? There are several."

"The one…ugh, looks about the size of this damn element in my hands." Usually lifting heavy objects didn't tax him. Though the cybernetic limb had even more strength, the nanites in their systems gave him and the other cyborgs in Full Throttle more strength than the average human.

She shifted from foot to foot, peering into the bed of the hauler, shifting the tarp around.

"Could you hurry?"

Her mouth formed a tiny O, and she tossed the tarp completely off, grabbed the platform and jogged over to him. "You could have said the thing that looks like a box but isn't a box. That would have made more sense."

She set the platform at his feet, and he carefully maneuvered the element onto it.

"You could have just grabbed the black object that looked to be the same size. Jesus, you find excuses for everything."

She frowned and crossed her arms. "It's not an excuse. I'm a fan of clear communication."

"Well, let's clear this up then." He motioned between them, despising how the lower part of his anatomy appreciated those wind-swept curls and the sheen of perspiration on her forehead. "I'm real good at looking and not touching. You would benefit from the same."

"You arrogant sonuva—"

"And you might want to grab that tarp the wind's about to carry away. That's what's going to keep you from spending the night on the cold hard ground."

She spun around and took off on a dash, swearing as she went. The panic in her face, the mad flail of her arms and legs toward the tarp, had Jack almost in tears and his belly hurting from laughing so much.

He set the solar panels in place, opened the element up, exposing the coils, and flipped the switch. The element hummed to life, a noise that meant warmth would soon be theirs. Hard to believe people used to burn things as a source of fuel. Technology allowed them to use smaller engines, similar to those on the ships, to spread heat and electricity to others. Bone powder fueled them, in small quantities. Nothing like what a ship would power. Five grams could fuel a whole gang-town for months.

"That's it!" Shannon all but hurled the tarp at him, the corner of the woven plastic sheeting hitting him in the face. "I need a drink. Tell me you packed something of the shine or ale variety."

Jack shook his head as he folded the tarp up. "Nope, water only this trip. No sense drinking on a job. We can't afford to be caught unaware. Especially going into unknown territory."

"Unbelievable. I'm on a trip with a member of the Mars Protectorate. You're a killjoy, Jack."

He almost took offense at being compared to those stick-up-the-ass jerks that worked for the Mars Commission, but he firmly believed in being safe. "I'm responsible."

"Being responsible only ever got someone bored. You finish the camp. I'm going to the checkpoint bar."

"I don't think —"

"That's right, you don't. I do. And, I say it's worth a little reconnaissance. Know what we are traveling into over the border. See if there are any new disputes between gangs. Possible slither sightings. We need to be at our best. I won't get that info huddling next to you."

He wanted to argue against the idea, but there was a glint to her gaze that said she was set in her mind to do this. Any rebuttal would only fuel her fire. *Just like my mom.* "Fine, do what you want. I'm about finished anyway. Should I prepare dinner?"

"I'll get something there," she said, already walking away and waving off his concern. He watched her for a minute as she headed off, tempted to go with her.

Being in a room full of people would be far better than being left alone with his thoughts, with the growing realization that soon he might not even be able to lift the element at all. Or have control over his body, not just his leg.

Keep working.

That was the way to fend off horrible thoughts and ideas. He made a meal out of dried meat, a bread packet which coagulated with fresh water into a dumpling the size of his palm and seasoned vegetables, vacuum sealed for freshness. Hell, Rune had packed pickled carrots too. It was like a little feast just for him.

He enjoyed the food, paying attention to the noises. A few howls in the distance, a soft breeze, the chilly night air.

Anything to keep his focus from the potential of what would happen with failure of this mission. He gathered the tarp under his head and lay at the entrance to the tent to stare at the stars and get the blankets warm in front of the element before moving them inside the tent.

They couldn't fail at this chance to cure the nanites, but trusting Shannon…

"Jack!"

His name was like a long cry on the wind. Funny how her voice carried to him like an audible mirage. He was damn tired, starting to imagine her crying out.

"Jack, we have to go!" Closer, louder.

Jack sprang up onto the balls of his boot-encased feet. Shannon was running toward him, panting, her eyes wide as she glanced over her shoulder in the direction of the checkpoint then back again.

He groaned. "What happened?"

"We have to leave now!"

Dust kicked up around and behind Shannon as she ran. She didn't head for the tent, but the hauler.

She dared to look again. At least four of the ten that had been in the bar had followed. She'd planned on one drink, maybe two. Ask the locals about the latest news. Sell her story as a long-lost Zephyr returning to the roost.

Then had come the offer of a card game. A little rum-running. It had been called another name once upon a time on Earth, but the goal was always to get more throuples of suits or numbers on the table than the other person.

And you never know when to stay no.

"Jack, what the hell are you doing?" She focused back on him as she climbed into the hauler's driver seat.

Instead of getting his ass to the vehicle as requested, Jack had the tarp and a blanket draped over one shoulder and was struggling to move fast with the heating element in both hands.

"Damn it." She hopped out and helped him. The damn man shouldn't have been lifting heavy things to begin with, and she'd remember that for the future.

Once the element was in the bed of the hauler and Jack had covered it with the tarp, he turned to head back to the tent.

She snagged him by the arm and pulled with all her strength. It barely stopped him. "What are you doing?"

"The tent? The food stores? We need those."

The angry voices were closer. A pistol shot fired and the laser bolt carrying it hit the tent dead on. The electricity caused enough of a spark to catch the fabric on fire.

"Looks like they just solved the dilemma for us. We have to leave, Jack. Right now or this mission ends before it begins."

He growled. "Fine."

Scrambling into the hauler, she ended up in the driver's seat, being on that side of the vehicle. More laser bolts whizzed right over head. One hit the door of the hauler with a screech of electricity against metal.

Thank heavens it didn't get through. Too close.

"Yikes, let's roll." She put everything in gear and took off. *Here's hoping what supplies we still have are bolted down.*

Ten solar minutes later, the checkpoint was long gone and they were officially in Auster territory.

"Do you mind telling me now what the hell happened?"

Chapter Eight

Familiar sights were already assailing her. The rock formations she'd seen any number of times on trips to the checkpoint to sell Zephyr goods and steal from visitors. Yeah, her family and her friends weren't the most honest.

The direction they had headed in was the right one. Their only problem was they couldn't drive all night. She was exhausted. The four drinks she'd slung back of that corn mash weren't helping either.

"A misunderstanding is what happened." She kept her foot on the accelerator, feeding a steady stream of fuel to the hauler's engine.

"I think we're well out of range you can quit speeding across open plains. We don't need to hit something."

She let out an uneasy breath. Her heart was still pounding in her chest. If she spoke her true feelings, Jack would think she was crazy, but she'd never felt so alive. "Another reason I'm driving. Auster doesn't have all the wildlife."

"Then what about that rock?"

Shannon immediately started to slow down, steering the hauler out of the way of the giant boulder dead center in their path. "Exactly why driving at night isn't ideal."

"We can slow down any time you want, and you can explain yourself. Since we just lost almost a week's worth of supplies and our tent." The low tone of Jack's voice and the way he kept his hand locked on the frame of the hauler door were clear signs his patience was waning.

She kept driving, her hands gripping the steering wheel tight. "Like I said, they misunderstood. I went in for a drink and then a couple of the men offered to let me in on their card game. A little friendly betting, drinks and whatnot. I won a few rounds and naturally it made sense to raise the wager."

"To what? You don't have anything to trade."

And she never did. "That's why I don't lose."

"But if they were chasing you…"

"I never said I don't cheat. I said I don't lose." And that was how she'd been found out. "A card slipped out of my sleeve at an inopportune time and those idiots were less forgiving. Even though one of them was pulling a swindle, too. Better to follow the crowd."

Jack scoffed. "So, then you led them to our campsite."

"Where else was I supposed to go? I didn't have any weapons on me. I'm not exactly built to take on four grizzled, beefy men."

She dared a glance at him, only to see him scowling at her in turn. "If you're willing to wage a battle, then you need to be prepared to fight it."

Shannon did her best to keep from smiling, clamping her lips together. But she had to ask. "Who told you this word of wisdom?"

"My father. A good man, with a good heart. He believed you fought the battles you chose."

Fathers... Shannon's opinion of them lay firmly within the definition of the word worthless. "Mine believed you steal, stab or cower from them. Let's just say I'm not a fan of those three, but I do believe in surviving."

A flash of light in the sky to their left caught her eye, and a glance at the clouds racing toward them had her searching for cover.

She caught sight of a cliff face in the distance, one that might have a cave or two. They just needed somewhere to keep safe. When she compressed the accelerator, the hauler sped up.

"Thought we agreed driving slower would be ideal."

"No can do, Deputy Jack. There's a storm headed this way." She pointed over her shoulder at the mess barreling their direction. She didn't miss Auster thunderstorms, especially night ones. Being raised a Zephyr, there were always warnings about getting caught above ground after dark.

Though she'd once risked it and gotten a wicked set of bruises on her legs and back from being pelted by the ice crystals raining down.

"It's a light rainstorm, nothing to be scared of. If anything, we'll get a free shower."

Shannon scoffed. "You are definitely a Wespero through and through. Auster region doesn't get your light showers. Not during this part of the year. The rotation of the planet, relation to the sun...even the terraforming couldn't have predicted this mess. Night storms here typically involve something we call razors."

"Razors?" The tone of his voice matched the one-eyebrow-lifted stare he tossed her way.

"Little balls of ice. They cut like the sharpest knife on exposed skin, burn a little too. On covered skin they leave nasty bruises and that's if you're lucky. Grown men cry after getting hit with this stuff. If they get big enough, they can even go through metal, wood... anything."

"Then we need cover, fast."

Now he's getting it.

She pointed out over the dash. "See that cliff face. There is bound to be a cave or two we can take shelter in."

"If we're hiding there, won't other animals be as well?"

Maybe she didn't give Jack enough credit. He had a sharp mind when put to a task. "It's possible, but you have the heating element so we should be able to scare most of them away."

A lie, but one she'd tell to keep them on this path. There could be a slither in there or a half dozen other things. There was a reason she'd chosen to wander Wespero and not her home territory after ditching Kascade's failed plan.

Lightning flashed across the sky and for a moment she got a better look at the rock wall they approached.

Her stomach tightened as she glimpsed an open maw of a cave.

She'd lived for years in the darkness of the hollowed-out, underground paths of her gang-town. The moonies' compounds on Earth's moon weren't much different. Monsters could hide in either place.

But I'm a monster, too.

Wind whipped up, blowing Shannon's curls every which way. She slammed her foot on the accelerator willing the damn hauler to move faster with every atom in her body.

"Shit, it's picking up quick." Jack glanced over his shoulder, eyes wide at whatever he saw.

She refused to look. "We're almost there."

The first razors hit, small like tiny needles digging into her shoulders.

No way do I go out like this.

"You need to slow down. We can't approach a pitch-dark space like this."

"Too bad," she replied right as they entered the cave. Only after they passed the entrance did she slam on the brakes. The headlights gave enough illumination for her to see a tire-killing rock and avoid it with a modest swerve. The movement was enough to get the hauler in a spin thanks to the loosely packed sand beneath the wheels.

The brakes started to jam and she eased off before slamming on them again. She winced at the grinding noise and Jack cursed repeatedly until they finally came to a halt, facing the opening they'd arrived through. Outside, the storm had hit with a ferocity of blinding razors, wind and lightning. The ground was covered in thousands of tiny balls. The beams from the headlights failed to cut through the tempest.

"See? Safe and sound."

Jack glowered at her. His blond eyebrows bunched, and his eyes narrowed. She could only imagine how much he wanted to hurt her, though his fierce expression seemed to arouse her more than anything.

Not heading toward seduction territory again.

"I wouldn't call this safe."

"This storm is probably hitting the checkpoint too. We're actually lucky we got out when we did. That shoddy tent of yours would have never held up to the razors."

Jack hopped out of the hauler and immediately started digging in the storage bed. "Funny, you didn't mention any of these possibilities before we left Frog Lick. Additionally, you admitted what I've been saying to everyone all along…you're a cheat."

He produced a handheld light and switched it on. The bright beam hit her square in the eyes. "The fuck? Can you watch where you point that?"

The beam swept away toward the right, Jack resituating his body to look behind the hauler as Shannon rubbed away the stars in her eyes.

"I'm not a cheat…I'm just not a loser."

"Phrasing it differently doesn't change your actions." He took a few steps deeper into the cave until he stood a couple feet away from the end of the hauler. "There doesn't appear to be any residents here at the entrance, but the cave is fairly deep. I'd recommend we don't go any further."

Shannon didn't disagree with the suggestion. She exited the hauler and moved toward the heating element. "Then let's get this block out and fired up."

They worked together, Shannon trying not to appreciate the flex of Jack's biceps as they set up the heating element. She also refused to continue talking about her penchant for cheating at card games.

Any game, be honest with yourself. "*If life wasn't meant to be cheated, then we wouldn't be given the opportunity.*"

Kascade had said that to her in one of his more vulnerable moments — when he'd dropped the façade of leader to the future of humanity, and embraced the fact he was still bitter about his daughter's death. Shannon had been dumb enough to get caught up in that mess. Dumb to believe people did more for others than just use them. So, she had learned to use them back.

My father turned out to be right about one damn thing.

"There's a cord missing...damnit." Jack started to toss things around in the back of the hauler, his movements more erratic by the second. Shannon walked over and took a minute to grab the handheld light and sweep the back seat.

A thin, black cord lay across the floor of the hauler and Shannon snatched it up before popping into a standing position and shouting, "Found it!"

Jack's gaze narrowed and Shannon angled the light beam on the triple pronged metal end of the cord. "That's three, this is two."

"Easily fixed." Shannon shoved the handheld under her arm and applied pressure to the third prong with both her thumbs.

"Wait!"

"It will take two seconds —"

"No, that goes..." The third prong snapped off and fell to the ground. "To something else."

"Well, now it's going to go into the heating element so we can connect to the hauler and not risk running out of heat." Because damn if she wasn't almost shivering. The storm had dropped the temperature even further.

Jack snatched the cord from her hand. "Fine. Get those extra blankets out and cover up. Sit on the ground, close to the back tire, and I'll finagle this."

There was no sense in arguing, not when the adrenaline of their chase and escape was wearing off. Her legs ached, her eyes itched and now that the idea of sitting had been introduced into her brain, her body refused to entertain any other thought besides getting off her feet.

Immediately after putting her back against the tire of the hauler, she shut her eyes. The blanket offered little warmth, and she shivered furiously even as Jack moved the element into position.

A few minutes later, something large and warm bumped up against her. She jerked out of instinct.

"Whoa, it's me." Jack's voice was low, soothing, as if he meant to provide comfort and reassurance. "Lean up against me. You're freezing."

People didn't do that. "You're too nice, Jack."

"A personal failing most folks I know don't complain about...yet, this is the first time you've thought that way."

She smiled and briefly opened her eyes only to find his gray stormy ones staring back at her, mere inches away. "Because this is the first time you've ever been nice to me."

"There's a reason for that," he replied in a barely there whisper.

The storm still raged outside, closing them off from the world at large, the mission. Exactly why she felt like she could push this topic further.

"Oh, what reason?"

The answer hovered there, unspoken. But instead of having the balls to say anything, Jack cleared his throat and adjusted his pants. Shannon toyed with the idea of reaching for him, sealing her lips to his, snaking a hand up his thigh and seeing if he'd gotten hard sitting so close to her.

"Shannon?"

"Hmm?" She took a gander at his lips now, full and lush. He had the presence of good bone structure, though up close she could see a few faded scars, one on his cheek and another on the side of his nose.

"I asked you to tell me more about your gang-town. Where you come from?"

She frowned. The last thing she wanted to talk about was her past life, the life they were headed toward. "Does it matter?"

"Every person's point of origin story matters." There was an innocent quality to his response. This hopeful idea people were important. *Outside of their bones, not so much.*

"This one doesn't."

Chapter Nine

They were stuck in a cave, had lost their food stores and tent and been chased across the rough terrain thanks to her reckless behavior. Jack had been pissed at Shannon. Her lack of information, her risky actions, cheating…and yet. When he'd seen her propped against the hauler, her eyes closed, her plump lips turning blue and those curls vibrating against her shoulders as she shivered, something inside his chest reacted as if punched.

He found himself desperate to get her warm.

Be close to her.

Then he'd sat beside her and he could see the cord to the necklace, his charm hanging from her neck. He'd meant to provide comfort…until she'd looked at him as if she wanted to eat him.

He needed to keep this line drawn. Not engage with her and focus on the end goal. Implementing a distraction came next and while successful, he despised how she put herself down.

"Let me be the judge of that."

Her frown deepened and he almost laughed at the little indents that appeared on her forehead above her eyes. He filed those details away, the same with the rich dark brown color of her curls. They looked black in this low light with a glimmer of red from the element. He was tempted to touch them... He had before and they were as soft as he'd imagined. *Shit.*

"It's easy." He had to try to get some sort of conversation going. "Start with your gang-town name."

"Zephyr."

He paused, mouth open, amazed she'd responded. "All right, and what's Zephyr like?"

She shook her head, those curls bouncing with the light movement. "Nothing like Frog Lick. We don't live above ground in Auster. Sure, there are a few buildings, for appearances sake, and trade meetings. But our strongholds exist below ground. Miles of tunnels, living spaces and gathering areas. Plenty of storage space, and our mining operations are more a part of daily life since we're so close."

The concept thrilled and terrified him. Cities below ground seemed far more advanced than those in Wespero could have imagined.

"Why below ground?"

She pointed toward the cave entrance where the razors had slowed, the wind starting to howl less. "Those storms were a big motivator."

"Makes sense. And your parents?"

All emotion left her face, her expression blank. "I don't think I'm up for talking anymore. How about we try to sleep?"

"Touchy topic, I get it. I don't think anyone on Mars can claim to have perfect parents." He patted his shoulder. "You can lean against me."

The only way they'd get through this adventure was to build trust. Shannon appeared to prefer hiding, whether internally or externally. She liked her secrets, her cheats and games. Continuing to entertain those would put Jack's life on the line more so than it had been already.

And I need to know if she's it.

"Fine." She gently rested her head against him. "But I'm still not talking about them."

Jack bit his lip to stop from smiling. "I'm not going to force you to. Just share a bedtime story. I was born in Frog Lick, grew up there. Never traveled anywhere besides racing domes. My father was a miner. Hardcore labor, hauling the rocks to process the Marsanium. My mother…"

Shannon's eyes were closed, breathing even, but not asleep. "Your mother what?"

Maybe if I tell her she'll be willing to open up. "She was a drunk and gambled away everything we owned repeatedly. My father would stop her, and she'd try for a bit, but would always return to the gambling, the games, and ultimately didn't care what happened as long as she got a drink. She drowned in the booze, stating without it she hated her life, her husband, me…that she'd never been given the opportunity for more."

"At least she was honest…"

Jack stiffened at Shannon's words. They worked through him like a dull blade jaggedly cutting the muscles in his chest.

She sighed, then continued. "You knew she didn't love you. The only thing we can be thankful for is people being truthful about their hate. Though you didn't deserve her censure. Whereas I deserved every bit of hate they tossed my way."

Her tone was all matter-of-fact, her body completely at ease against him. No shudder of emotion, no tears or clenching of her fists. She accepted the words she spoke as truth.

All the pain Jack suffered morphed into sympathy for this woman who obviously believed herself the worst and embraced those ideas to her core.

"No one deserves that."

"Shush. I'm done pouring my heart out. We won't have long before dawn and I get cranky with no food." Her eyes stayed shut, and Jack let his gaze drift across their surroundings. The weakening storm, the heating element with its red coils, the wall of rock around them and the woman against him.

Her grav boots were worn, small holes visible, her cargo pants patched in various places. She had come to them broken, needing flash and trading her knowledge to survive. There were so many like her, on the brink of losing a never-ending battle in a universe that offered no one favors. But his brothers had offered him a chance to fight against circumstance.

Maybe I can give her one.

* * * *

The ground shimmying beneath him shook him awake. His sharp jolt earned him a punch to the shoulder from Shannon.

"Quit moving." She resituated herself, snaking her arm around his torso and gripping him tight.

When did that happen?

Hell, a glance downward and she wasn't on his shoulder anymore. No, the majority of her body was draped over his chest, with the blanket covering them both.

The heating element had died at some point. The coils were no longer illuminated red. Sunbeams filtered in through the cave entrance, though the air temperature was still cool.

Jack dared to let himself feel Shannon against him. Her body heat, the rise and fall of her chest as she breathed. A few stray curls had fallen over her face. He brushed those aside. When was the last time he'd slept with a woman?

Never…because sex isn't sleeping.

No, Jack preferred his own space for sleep. He tended to believe it was the last sacred thing he could share with the person he was meant to be with.

Those curls out of the way, Jack saw the medallion, closer than ever.

It's mine. She's mine. Shit.

"One day it will return to you…"

He rubbed his fingertips together to stifle the urge to touch the piece of bone he'd carved the indentations on.

Shannon groaned beneath him, then stretched. Her hand brushed his groin and he stifled a moan with a cough.

She sat up, acting as if nothing had happened. Shrugging off the blanket, she tucked her necklace under her shirt. "What time is it?"

"Not sure, but from the angle of the sun it's probably closer to mid-afternoon."

Shannon stood up and stretched again, this time revealing pale flesh and a belly button with a wicked scar trailing up her stomach. "We slept too long then. The next town is a good clip. How long until you can be ready?"

So fast and abrupt. He was still reeling from the marrow-deep revelation he'd discovered when he woke with her sleeping on him.

"Jack, you okay?" With no hesitation, she was on her knees beside him, checking his pulse. "Pain in your leg? I didn't put too much pressure on it sleeping next to you, did I?"

The questions overwhelmed his senses, along with her proximity. He couldn't stop himself from trying to look everywhere at once, from his skin tingling and his hands once again yearning to grab for her. She'd been a dream, a myth, and now she was real.

You're a fool.

"I'm fine." He threw his hands up as he spoke, putting a halt to her examination. "Just shaking off the rust. Give me five solar minutes. Then I'll pack up the element, check the hauler and we can go."

Five minutes turned into an hour as they had to put the hauler into neutral and push it out of the cave into the sunlight. The solar power needed to regenerate. They'd drained the battery running the element all night.

In turn, he wore himself out. His leg screamed in pain.

"Get in the hauler and I don't mean the driver seat." Shannon opened the door to the passenger side and pointed.

Jack grimaced as he hobbled his way there, gripping the side of the hauler for support. "It's getting worse."

"More like you pushed yourself too far."

He climbed into the seat and used his hands to lift his leg inside. "This is embarrassing."

"Imagine how I feel? We roll into the next town and I'm helping a messed-up driver out of vehicle. You're ruining my credibility." She flicked her wrist and brushed her hair over her shoulders before slamming the door shut.

"You've got cred in this shithole region?"

She laughed at him, the unabashed sound echoing back into the cave. He would have traded whatever she asked for to hear it over and over again. "There, it worked. Took your mind off the pain. Let's get moving."

* * * *

The sun had already started to fall by the time they reached the closest sign of civilization. Sounds of music, laughter and a few engine revs hit his ears. His stomach growled so loud it could have competed with the engine.

"Looks like we made it in time to feed the beast."

Jack didn't mention how if Shannon had stayed at the campsite the night prior, they wouldn't be in this predicament with no food and barely any water. His urge to say anything came from being uncomfortable and pissed that he had to rely on Shannon for help.

His leg didn't hurt nearly as bad as earlier and he focused on grounding himself in their current surroundings. The gang-town they'd driven into wasn't like others. There were mounds of hardened mud built up, at least seven feet high, every ten feet or so. Twelve in all. Each one had a rickety wooden door facing the trodden, dirt-packed street. No windows, no roofs, with cacti plants lining the sides of each one to prevent people from climbing atop them.

The only building with a similar construction to those in Frog Lick lay at the far end of the street, a two-story structure of thick logs, a mud-packed roof and a dead end that everyone eventually would run into. There were barbed-wire fences along the sides trailing back to the mud mounds.

A cliff face wasn't too far behind the building and Jack imagined there was a cave there too.

"I take it those mounds are housing?"

Shannon shrugged. "Maybe…they could be buildings used for different purposes, but you can bet they connect to a structure underground. The tall two-story ahead is going to be their version of the Watering Hole. But more like a place to get food, drink, supplies and trade."

"All-in-one?"

"Auster gangs don't like anyone having too much access to their places. You'll find every gang-town out here has the one place for visitors to congregate. Try to go anywhere else and you're likely to end up never seeing the surface again." Shannon's point got hammered home as they got further down the would-be street, closer to the all-in-one. Several armed men and women stepped out from the mounds, menacing gazes turned on them.

Jack returned their stares with one of his own, sitting up straight in his seat. He'd been raised on this godforsaken planet, too. His tough guy persona could be backed up.

Shannon cleared her throat. "Nice rough front, but maybe tone it down a bit. Don't want to get us kicked out before we even ask for food."

Jack kept his scowl in place, even thumped his hand on the dash as they passed another couple who'd emerged from the last mound. They jumped. "If you were born on Mars, then you know why I can't do that. It's not in our blood to submit to anyone outside of our gang leader."

She scoffed. "Well, then don't start complaining when our next encounters are less than smooth. Hell, I'll let you go in first and initiate negotiations."

The hauler came to a stop right in front of the two-story trading post. Suddenly the loud voices and the rambling music struck Jack wrong. Odd, because he'd always been the driver assigned to trading runs. Had always found a woman or two who liked to entertain him on his travels.

In this exact moment, all the confidence he normally would have had in this same situation drained away. He didn't want to walk in there by himself, at the mercy of folks who might've heard about the incident at the border checkpoint.

"You okay over there?" Shannon asked as she turned the hauler off.

The grin and the mischievous glint in her gaze bothered the hell out of him.

He hunched his eyebrows and huffed twice for good measure. She'd played him again, over and over like she was tuning up engine pistons with a little grease. No more doubting himself. He had to quit letting her get in his head to break his resolve. He had enough to deal with.

"Yeah, tired of your games, though. I've handled plenty of trades, buys and any number of negotiations over the years."

Shannon gave a slow nod. "Good, then get to it. While you get us something to eat, I'll ensure our hauler doesn't get stolen."

"Don't you trade a thing."

She winked in return, twisting her head away right after so those damn curls bounced. "I won't have to."

Jack opened the hauler door and took a deep breath as he prepared to stand up, nervous that he'd put weight on the damn metal leg only to have it give out from underneath. It wouldn't help his image with the people watching.

Don't fail me now, nanites.

Grabbing ahold of the door for leverage, just in case, he pulled himself to a standing position, trying his best to keep the bulk of his weight on his human leg. He evened things out slowly until he was sure the cybernetic limb wouldn't give way, then slammed the door shut.

Jack took his time walking away from the hauler. A slow, easy stride to ensure he didn't fall flat on his face and put on a show for the locals. He made it inside and liked how there was no sudden stop to anything at his entrance.

For the most part, those inside the Trading Post ignored him. They were gathered around tables, listening to the guitarist strumming out a rhythm in the far corner, playing games of chance with cards or dice and throwing darts.

He walked straight over to the bar and luckily found a pair of unoccupied stools. The others nearby gave him a once over, but mainly because his metal leg clinked with each step. He usually kept it pretty well lubricated to ensure silence, but the last forty-eight hours had Jack forgoing a lot of his normal practices.

Gotta fix that later.

He slid onto the bar stool and tapped on the roughened, weary bar top. There were gashes cut into it, names carved, a sign of longevity and disrespect. No one would've attempted such a thing in Frog Lick. Gaia would have stabbed them if they did.

"Can we get you something?" The man who approached had long gray hair, an unkempt beard, leathered skin and glassy eyes. Older than dirt, which was surprising, because long lives weren't something Mars promoted.

"Looking for a couple glasses of recycle and maybe a bowl of whatever stew you have."

Glassy-Eyes snorted. "Stew…we serve a slice of bread with a smear of fat and you can get a side of boiled roots or we've got a broth. No meat in these parts, not unless you got flash…but those asking for recycle…"

"We're passing through headed for Zephyr. Storm last night took most of our supply, but I can pay." Jack refused to lay out how much crinkle he was willing to part with. The amount he had was more than he'd ask Drag to give him, but the leader of Full Throttle wanted to put Jack in a position that wouldn't leave him stuck.

"Well, that changes things a bit. I'll give you a loaf, a canister of recycle, a bottle of shine and even a box of BCS-issue protein cubes for five ounces."

Might end up there anyway.

"Five ounces…that's robbery even by bootlegger standards."

"He's right." Shannon's voice washed over him, making his skin break out in chill bumps. She slid onto the stool next to him. "You're trying to rip us off, old-timer."

Glassy-Eyes held up his hands in mock surrender. "Those are the prices. I just set 'em based on supply and demand. Old philosophy if you're short on goods, can't make money, you raise prices."

Shannon leaned up against the bar. "Then how about a bet?"

No might about it—she'd get them caught for sure. Jack was screwed.

Chapter Ten

Shannon pointed in the direction of the dart board against the wall to the right of them. "I make that bullseye in less than three shots and you give us everything you said for free."

The Old Beard grinned, showing his scraggly teeth were chipped, decaying or missing. "And when you don't?"

He'd been in this dumb town since she was little and he liked bartering in stupid ways more than he enjoyed making money. She remembered her father arm-wrestling for a box of parts once.

"Don't do something so stupid." Jack scowled at her, his gaze pointed.

If she could read his mind, it might have been complaining about how her gambling had gotten them in this situation in the first place. But yesterday was different...and she didn't make bets she couldn't win.

She winked in Jack's direction then looked back at Old Beard. "What do you think is a fair price?"

"You pay me double for wasting my time. I could be pouring drinks for paying customers." Old Beard jerked his head toward the others sitting down the opposite end of the bar. "They don't try to lie to men. They're too far gone for nonsense."

Shannon laughed. "Oh, but you're not willing to say no? We don't have to go through with anything."

Old Beard pointed his towel at her. "See, you're trying to back out. You know you can't."

This was how the Argest trader worked, but he wasn't as good as he used to be back in her youth. He'd grown too old for this, but no doubt refused to give up his spot. Someone would kill him for it at some point, especially if they believed the gang wasn't seeing enough profits.

"No way. I'm in this. Tell them, Jack, how good I am."

"She's ridiculous. Can make it two shots not three." Jack's monotone voice didn't faze her. She'd get him to play along if it killed her. He needed to cut loose a little more, especially in the face of an uncertain tomorrow. *I go down my way.*

She glanced back at him, mouth open in mock outrage. "Don't tell them *all* my secrets. A woman's got to have a few."

Rolling her shoulders, she stood up from the stool, deliberately letting the legs scratch against the floor. The sharp sound flooded the room, even competing with the mellow drone of a guitar. Several pairs of eyes focused on her from the bar and the surrounding tables.

"All right, Old Beard, I'm going to show you how darts should be thrown." She cracked her knuckles, stretched her arms and legs, drawing out the show.

The darts were handed to her by another bystander. He looked her over with one yellowed eye, but the skinny husk of a man wasn't anything attractive. The other eye was covered in a patch and his dry flaked skin showed signs she'd seen before on those who abused the bottle.

"You get it in two, I'll throw myself in for the night," the bystander said.

A sharp scrape rent the air, along with the familiar clink of Jack's cybernetic leg. "She's not in need of any companions for the night," he hollered.

Shannon grinned and glanced back at Jack who was standing, arms crossed, glowering. "He's right. I already have one."

Grabbing the darts from Eye Patch's hand, she stepped up to the carved mark in the wood flooring. The dart board was three feet away.

"Do I just throw when I want to or am I getting a countdown?"

Her skin prickled, the little hairs rising up on her arms and the back of her neck. So many folks watching, people curious at the ongoings, others knowing Old Beard was up to his tricks. She needed to nail this. She would hit the target.

I've got no choice.

Never had a choice to fail, because failure meant she'd be giving into someone else. Taking a deep breath, she put the first dart in her left hand. A bend at the elbow, a cock of the wrist, positioning the dart rod between her thumb and index finger, and a couple fake pumps before she let the dart fly.

It whistled through the air, reminding her of her adopted mother's tea kettle that would howl once the water heated up, or the sound of an arrow being hurled at her head.

The dart landed halfway between the bullseye and the edge. A mixture of cheers and jeers erupted in the Trading Post, Old Beard being the loudest of them. "Keep throwing them like that and I'll be the one eating good tonight."

"I've got two more darts. Just calm down." She smiled, wiped her forehead with her forearm and tried to force away the memory of her father.

He didn't deserve space here, even if he was the reason she'd gotten so good at judging distances. She'd tried her best to take every mean thing he'd done to her and turn it into a strength.

No weaknesses. The second dart sailed even wider. The sound was duller, less sharp...as intended.

"You sure you want to keep going?" One eye asked, doing a triple take at the board.

Doubt...she'd lived with it her entire life.

There was a hand on her shoulder. The weight seemed familiar, the callused touch warm and catching on the fabric of her shirt.

"Maybe we should back out."

"Get out of here, Jack. Too late now. Don't you all have a fancy catchphrase or something... Dust or bust?" She spoke low, frustrated that even he had bought into the act. She'd become damn good at her sell.

He still stood there, giving her an indecipherable look, scrutinizing her in a way she found a little disturbing, as he took in every aspect of her from the way she held the last dart to her neck. *What the hell?*

"I'm not quitting. I don't bet —"

"Unless you can win." He grinned at her then, randomly trailing a finger along the rope of her necklace, before lifting the charm from under her shirt and sending it twirling. She wasn't ready for the flutter that erupted inside her with the flash of his pearly whites or the familiarity to his actions. "Just hurry up, I'm hungry."

She looped her arms around his neck and played one step further. "For food or something else?"

He blushed. *Holy shit*. She made his skin flush red and it disappeared under the collar of his shirt.

"Oye! I'm not betting for a sex show. Stow the touchy-feely and throw the dart," Old Beard hollered, effectively ruining the moment.

But the bulge in Jack's pants currently pressing against her stomach would be worth investigating later. "Guess I better get to it," she whispered to Jack. Then she let him go and looked back at Old Beard. "Tell you what, let's up the bet one more time?"

"You prove you can even make the shot first."

Enough playing. She stepped back up to the line, angled her arm and let loose. The dart hit dead center and every voice in the post went silent. The only thing Shannon could hear was the single strum of a guitar string.

"Willing to bet I can't make the shot again?" Shannon made sure her voice was nice and loud so everyone heard.

Old Beard stroked said beard. "What do you want if I say yes?"

"A bed for the night. I know you have rooms upstairs." She'd stayed in one with her father when a storm kicked up during one of their trade runs. They needed to get a good night's rest, for the sake of Jack's left leg. At least that was the excuse she'd tell anyone who asked. If she could win instead of paying for it, all the better.

"No way she can make it a second round." This came from the one-eyed scummer who had handed her the darts in the first place.

She ignored the accompanying agreements from others in the room and kept her gaze on Old Beard.

"You miss and I get the nice hauler you parked out front."

Jack shook his head, the confidence he'd granted her earlier melting under the pressure. She was tempted to back away simply to spare Jack the anxiety attack he was probably experiencing. Except something moved deep within, this urge to show off and prove how she was still her own person even when she was at the mercy of others.

A grin and a wink, that was what she gave Jack in return. "It's a bet. Someone give me a dart."

One-Eyed Scummer produced another dart and Shannon accepted it with a little bow. Time to secure herself a mattress and pillow for the night. No hard ground, blanket and an element. She took less than ten seconds to calculate her shot, cocking her wrist a bit higher so the dart would come down on top of the other one.

Then she whistled sharply and let the pointed future fly. She'd taken a big risk, but that was how she treated every day, every situation. *Risk big, win big.* The dart sailed with the precision of a laser-punched hole into metal. It landed right in the bullseye and Shannon had to tense up her stance to keep from jumping into the air. Winning was fine, but gloating would only cause them more trouble.

A mixture of groans and disbelief echoed around her, the loudest being Old Beard. She pivoted on her heel and took a slow saunter back to her bar stool. Jack was shocked to silence, not even looking at her. She started to wonder if he'd watched her win or had been too afraid to try.

"All right, pay up. I won per the terms of the bet."

Old Beard faced away from her. When he turned back around, he slapped a key down on the bar top, attached to a piece of Marsanium beaten down into a ring, smooth and shiny. "Room's up the stairs and on the left. Got a relief room attached. Don't tear anything up or you pay for it. Get out after first light and I'll have someone bring up your food and drink."

Jack lifted his head as Shannon reached for the key. He stilled her. "What if we want the food now?"

"My word is good. Just like no one will touch your hauler. The Zephyr won fair and square. Shouldn't have let you bait me like that."

Shannon's shoulders locked up at the callback to her past. "How'd you know?"

"Ephraim's girl...the hair, never would forget it. Besides you got the same talent he had for throwing things, hitting targets." Old Beard's words cut deep. She was nothing like him...the man who'd blamed her for his wife's death. The one who'd called her a murderer in the first place.

"Well, I wouldn't know. Thanks, Old Beard." To Jack, she motioned to the stairs with her chin. "I'm headed up. Coming?"

She didn't wait for him to follow, just took off for the room, ready to get the hell out. If that old man remembered her, then likely others might. She didn't need rumors or her old nickname to get kicked up.

Might make things a little more challenging as they made their way toward Zephyr. The high she'd been riding from the close contact with Jack and nailing the board with those darts had all but faded as she trudged up the rickety wooden staircase to the weathered, red-painted door.

Heavy steps followed her. "Hey, Shannon, wait up a minute. What the bartender said…"

She paused, key turned in the lock. "I don't want to talk about it."

A gentle shove got the door to swing open and she stepped inside. The sun was near set, fading to a purple twilight illuminating the visible sky from the single window. A couple chairs with threadbare cushions, a rug, a small table to set food on or play a game. A heating element against the wall. But the big plus was the bed. Not some small single either. No, this bed could easily fit three. It was gigantic. This was what she remembered…with three pieces of the finest assembled cotton and soft foam cushions from the Upper planets.

There were a couple blankets on top and some pillows. She wanted to sink down on that glorious piece of comfort and never get up.

"This is why you were willing to bet the hauler."

"I don't bet if I can't win," she replied, never taking her eyes off the bed, even as an electric tension surged in the air around her as he came to stop at her side.

"Would have been nice to get a little more warning."

She chuckled and side-eyed him. "You need to learn to have fun. Live."

"You were betting every possible bit of wealth we have. It's hard to leave that in the hands of someone I barely know. The last time you risked for a win, we lost our tent, our food—"

"All right, I get it. But my latest achievement should more than make up for the error. Besides, we're a day's travel from our destination. If we leave at daybreak as our host instructed."

Jack always wore a bland expression with her, not enough smiles or views of the laugh lines around his mouth. Even now, as he looked at the bed, he seemed less than amused. "Am I going to be allowed to share that with you?"

"Plenty of room for the both of us," she replied, unable to stop smiling. Then she started to laugh, her entire body quaking with the hilarity of Jack's somber mood to the prospect of sharing a sleeping space.

"What's so funny?"

"You...we slept beside each other propped up against a hauler last night. Hard rocky ground leaving indents in our ass cheeks. Yet you look even less enthusiastic about laying down next to me in comfortable surroundings. And you were the one who only brought one tent."

He sighed, a big heavy thing that left a second layer of tension in the room. Then he faced her. She wouldn't look at him, a little flame of fear sparking inside her coupled with frustration because if he brought up her past again...

"My apprehension has nothing to do with you and everything to do with me."

She kept her lips sealed because bullshit. Men, women, all the same—everyone said it was them and not her, but in reality they hid their true feelings without the nuggets to confront them.

He touched her arm, at first barely there then with a little more grip. "Could you at least face me while I'm trying to come clean?"

"What are you talking about?" She angled toward him, reminded of the differences between them immediately. He was all light hair, tan skin, calluses, scars and rough work. She'd spent the majority of her years in space, was lighter toned, and she wasn't nearly as tall. No, he beat her there, too. Along with the muscles she wanted to frame with her hands, massage, and explore.

"We climb in that bed, the stiff wood you rubbed against downstairs will be right back and it's damn difficult to ignore this for a second night in a row. Especially when there's a comfortable area to spread out and explore. I could deny my attraction when the circumstances weren't ideal, but this is…" He rubbed a hand over his jaw where a shade more than stubble was now present after a couple days of travel.

Her mouth pursed in an 'O' shape. "Wait, you want me?"

Damn if I'm not twisting the hell out of this.

Jack had reached an impasse with himself somewhere between sitting at the bar watching Shannon throw that first dart and standing beside her at the end of the bed they'd have to share. His attraction wasn't something he could separate from the business part of this anymore.

Not when he'd held her in his arms for a brief moment or when she asked if he was hungry for something else. Hell, his mind had delved deep into his hedonistic dreams, urging him to speak up and ask for what he'd been denying himself.

She can't be trusted.

But sex wasn't about trust, was it? Not with his previous bed partners. Physical encounters were about pleasure, scratching an itch that his hand couldn't satisfy. But she wore his necklace and he had put a lot of daydreams over the years into the woman that would show up one day wearing his jewelry and wanting to claim him.

Shannon had not fit those dreams in the slightest. She wasn't homely, a little shy and sporting a bobbed hairstyle in the colors of the rainbow. The last one was a bit far-fetched, sure, but he'd always liked women with a secret wild side. Wild as in they painted their nails or had a piercing in a private place...not in the sense they might gamble away everything he had on his person for a comfy bed.

Still, he couldn't deny those curls, curves and her devil-may-care swagger got his cock hard and his pulse racing. He enjoyed the thrill of her putting on the show for everyone downstairs. She had executed that plan and owned the room. Even the guitarist had gone silent in anticipation of her final throw.

He was getting hard all over again at the memory of her hips beneath his hands, her arms around his neck and those luscious lips of hers. "Yeah, figured you gathered that answer on your own." He pointed to the floor.

"But..." She sputtered a bit, failing to make words. He liked the grav boot on the other foot for a minute. "You can't stand me. You told me nothing short of fuck off, without those exact words, but your eyes. You're always leaving when I'm showing up. Hemi even joked about how he's got no idea what I did to —"

"Enough." He pulled her toward him in the same second as he cut off her speech, tired of her rambling all the ways he'd acted an asshole in an attempt to prevent exactly what was about to happen next. "I'm going to kiss you now and this is your one chance to object."

She peered up at him, eyes wide, and licked her damn lips before she smiled. "I'm waiting."

He wanted to wipe that smile right off her face, ratchet her desire up so she'd be begging for him to pound her into the mattress. But Jack had learned one thing over the years…patience. So instead of giving into the very thing he wanted, to put them both out of their misery. He kissed her…on the forehead.

Then he let go of her and stepped back. "Think I'll check out that washroom, maybe freshen up a bit."

"Are you fucking kidding me?" Shannon stomped her foot on the floor. "You Full Throttle boys are being taught wrong if you think that's a kiss."

She surged for him, latching her arms around his neck, her legs around his waist, like a bob-tailed scratcher would to a fence post. Her mouth was on his in seconds and he leaned into it, hunching down to give her more access, powerless against the onslaught. As soon as they connected, every nerve in his body hummed to life like an element kicking on for the first time. He'd generate enough heat for the both of them.

He moaned, more like a whimper, as she traced the seam of his lips with her tongue, seeking entry. Shannon was a force of nature, as strong as any storm Mars could generate, and he gave her exactly what she sought.

Their tongues were magnets of differing polarities. One minute tangled, then retreating, only to be helpless to join up again. He was doing his best just to remain standing and hold strong while she plundered him like a thief, eager to take and take. Jack loved how she kissed him, anchoring her hands in his hair and scratched at his scalp.

She slowed her actions for a second to mumble, "Take us to the bed."

He moved then, cupping her ass in his hands as they continued to devour each other. This meeting of the flesh seemed personal yet so minuscule at the same time. When he was about to release her onto the mattress, she stopped kissing him.

"Nope, you're going to sit."

Jack turned and did as she asked, letting Shannon slide off him before he landed on the bed. It was surprisingly more comfortable than any other bed he'd been in. "What now?"

"I'm cleaning up first…or you can wait five minutes, strip and join me."

"I'll start counting silently right now."

She laughed and took off, running around the bed to the other side and through the open doorway. Jack saw the light go on. The ion generator was next, a steady hum, followed by the sounds of objects hitting the floor.

He was still riding the wave of the kiss. *Why did I think I wanted a meek girl?*

Another minute passed and he decided to toe off his boots, tucking the socks inside. Next the belt, the pants, the shirt. He'd walk in there naked as the day he was born, so that way they didn't have to waste time. But he was careful to tuck all his clothes and boots over by a chair, out of the way. In case they rushed back to the bed.

There went his imagination again, with two minutes left. He reached down and stroked his hard cock a couple times, her taste still on his lips. Officially, he'd lost his mind—he was standing in the middle of a room, butt naked and jerking off when she peeked around the washroom doorway.

"Hey, that's not right, starting this party without me. Five minutes is up, get in here." Shannon crooked a finger in his direction and like a driver in front of a waving green flag, he went.

As he crossed the threshold into the washroom, he noticed a standing shower with a curtain. A stone edging had been put between the shower and the rest of the room to keep the ions contained.

"Old Beard downstairs might get pissed if we use all the allotted energy," Shannon said as she placed her hand over his on his cock, stroking with him. "But I don't give a shit. Show me how you like it."

Jack surfaced out of his momentary lust-haze with Shannon touching him. "We don't need extra attention. I'll show you whatever you want—just get in the shower."

She pulled him along with her by his dick. Her grip was firm, the tension how he liked it. They got into the shower and she pushed him against the wall. Ions whizzed and buzzed around them in swirling streams, washing away the dust, the dirt and the grime of their two days of travel.

With Shannon facing him, he finally took a moment to take all of her in. Breasts with areolas much larger than a mouthful, and pinkish, too. Those distended nipples were tight. The thatch of hair between her legs, the curve of her hips… He acted on instinct and started to map his way over every inch of her body with his palms. Neck, collarbone, shoulders, the scar on her right arm, her belly with several more scars and of course the tops of her thighs, where a tattoo of a winged bird sat on each one, though they were morbid, one with an eye gouged out, another with its throat slit.

"Those tattoos?"

"Shh, I'm going to suck your dick now. I've been thinking about this since the first time you got mad at me." She sank to her knees in front of him and popped his cock into her mouth before he could object. He'd never met a woman eager to suck him off unless she was being paid flash. This was an anomaly and one he felt damn guilty of allowing to continue. Because if there was one other lesson he'd been taught growing up, it was that women deserved to be worshipped and treated as queens. They were the future of the human race—without women, men didn't exist. Therefore, women should come first.

"Shannon, aah—"

She deep-throated him right then, with a self-satisfied moan vibrating around his cock. Jack had to grab the damn wall, his hands sliding on the slick surfaces until he shoved them against the coated tiles with a slap and held on for dear life.

She kept working him until the tell-tale feeling creeped up his spine and the muscles in his legs tensed.

"Shannon, if you don't stop I'm going to…"

She stopped sucking, popping him out of her mouth, and gazed up at him with the most sultry hooded eyes he'd ever seen. Her lips glistened with moisture. "That's the plan."

"But…not without you first."

A light chuckle from her shocked him a bit, then she leaned in to lick the pre-cum off his tip. His cock couldn't even stop leaking when she laughed. "I'll let you deliver when I'm done."

He stopped her from getting her mouth on him again and went against his every desire, crouching down and picking her up. He enjoyed the little sound of surprise that emerged from her mouth at his sudden dominant move.

"Let me give us a way we both get what we want." Moving the shower curtain out of the way, he marched them out to the bed. Then he set her down and climbed on the mattress by himself, lying with his head on the pillows.

"Hop on up here and straddle me with that delicious pussy of yours, but do so with your face in the opposite direction. Then you can suck me off and I'll give you the same pleasure."

She crossed her arms. "Are you serious?"

"As a better on race day. I want your cum as much as you want mine." He needed to know what she tasted like, the essence of her. Wanted to feel her shake and come apart on top of him. Hell, he hoped she squeezed the fuck out of him with her thighs.

"Then who am I to deny you?" She jumped on top of him, carefully positioning herself. The center of her was right there, and he spread her wide with his thumbs.

She was wetter than a well-lubed engine, slick and ready for a tonguing.

"You're a real surprise, Jack."

"Just wait… I've got a few more prepared for you."

Chapter Eleven

Sore was one word for how Shannon's body felt the next morning. Deliciously sore. She'd woken to Jack bringing her to the height of orgasm again. Shocking after they'd exhausted each other the night before.

Then he'd moved off to the bathroom, got dressed and gone downstairs to retrieve their respective bags from the hauler.

"You shower first. Then I'll go." He tossed the bags on the floor and went to the table where the rest of the food and recycled water remained.

Shannon shucked the blankets and sheet off, revealing her naked form. "Or we could go together."

"You're insatiable." He didn't even look at her twice, just headed for the bathroom and disappeared out of sight.

She refused to feel embarrassed about wanting more from him, especially since they'd kept everything to the oral side of pleasure. Now she wanted physical penetration.

"You're right, and I'd love for you to cure this hunger of mine by impaling me on your cock." She jumped off the bed and dashed to the doorway, pausing there and doing her best to look sultry…a slight angle to her hip, one foot on her tip-toes, and flinging her hopelessly tangled curls over her shoulder.

Jack faced away from her, turning on the ion shower, then he glanced over his shoulder. "If that's what you want, then you better get over here quick or I might finish with my hand instead."

Who knew Jack could be fun? Last night he'd been full of ideas. From opposing ends in a race to the finish, to creative things one could do with fingers. He'd even smiled a time or two. When he dared to grin, he rendered her speechless.

Even now words failed her, but her feet had the right idea, strutting toward her end goal with sure steps. When she reached him, he pulled her into his arms and kissed her. If a deity did exist, then they'd gifted Jack Renfro with the ability to use his mouth in ways no mortal should be able to. She'd thought she had control, but no…not when he put his tongue to work and those soft, full lips of his. Far softer than they should have been.

She shuddered in his embrace as he ended the kiss.

"Sure you want my cock in you and not something else?"

"Yes," she mumbled, blinking her eyes to clear away the momentary lust-induced blank that wiped logical thought from her head. "I've seen how talented you are with your mouth. Now, show me what this part of you can do."

Stroking him was another thing she enjoyed. The way he pulsed in her hand, how the slightest touch from her evoked precum to spill out of the tip. A type of power she'd been surprised by, how sensitive he was to her touch.

"How do you want it?"

"Hmm." She was looking at his dick, nothing else and how her hand was so small wrapped around his length. She smeared that precum over the head with her thumb resisting the urge to drop to her knees then and there.

"From behind? Or do you want to look at me while I fuck you?"

Words had never had her queued up so hot before. She was torn by the possibilities both positions could bring. "Can we do both?"

He chuckled then she dared to meet his gaze again. A glimpse of joy on his face was something that seemed to make anything worth it. Stupid really, but the laugh lines on his face were a gift she'd attempt to gain over and over.

"If we had more time, sure. But, I distinctly remember Old Beard, as you called him, saying we needed to be out at daybreak. Time's about up. So, it's gonna be fast, hard and we're going to have to clean up at the same time. Choose now or I choose for you."

Why did that last sentence mean so much to her? How he gave her a choice, even when he could easily just tell her what would happen.

"Take me from behind."

The joy on his face melted away, replaced with a determined glint to his eye. "Then step inside the shower, face the ion wall and brace yourself."

In her entire sexual past, she'd never let another partner tell her what to do, but in this instance, at the gentle yet commanding tone of his, she'd do whatever he asked. Because he didn't demand, just directed as if telling someone how to complete a simple task. The same way he'd helped her learn how to hammer in tent stakes.

And now he's going to hammer me.

She vibrated with excitement, stepping into the shower and positioning herself as he'd asked. "I'm ready."

"Yes, you are. I'm so tempted to just eat your pussy again. I love the way you taste, how you clench your thighs around my head when you're ready to come." He slid a hand down her spine, and the contact lit every nerve in her body to a frenzy. Paired with his words, she was going to be dripping soon enough.

He framed her hip with that same hand, then she felt the blunt tip of him slide back and forth over her entrance. "You're so damn wet. I…"

"I'm protected. Don't worry. I received the same blockers they give away freely on the Uppers." The only damn good things those bastards… *Ooooh.*

She was filled in a second. He slid all the way in with little resistance and she lost her sense of self as he seated his hard length inside her. He was more than she'd expected or imagined. This was what she'd been missing, a good, hard… *Fuck.*

He pulled out then slammed back in, picking up the pace. When he'd said fast, rough… *He fucking means it.*

Each thrust brought her closer. He was hitting the right spot every time and also driving her toward the wall a little bit as well. She adjusted her hands to better brace herself and submitted to the onslaught, letting him seek relief from her body and in return give her enough pleasure to drown out everything else.

No worries about what today would bring. The debt she still needed to pay was a minuscule problem for another day when surrounded with this much sensation, tingles over every inch of flesh as the ions cleaned their skin of impurities and Jack found the spot that had her panting. "I'm going to come. Jack. Please."

"Beg again." He reached between them and rubbed her clit, flicking it with his index finger, and she bit her lip to keep from screaming. Her orgasm erupted and she came. Not her normal release either — no, she exploded, squirting her orgasm all over the floor.

"Joseph's balls," Jack swore then kept moving his cock, rubbing his hand all over her clit and her release. He spread it all over his hand. Then he tensed, and she dared to look over her shoulder.

She started to orgasm again, on a smaller scale, but nevertheless so turned on at Jack licking his palm, his fingers, coated in her. Then he came, pulling out as he did. Shannon didn't hesitate to return the favor, eager to taste the saltiness of him. She turned, dropped to her knees and finished him off, catching one spurt in mid-stream.

They were both greedy for each other and this was a miracle because she'd never met someone who found her hard-core orgasms attractive. Until now.

When they both finally finished their insane need to consume, he helped her to a standing position. They didn't speak as they let the shower remove what evidence remained of their coupling. Shannon found she enjoyed this momentary silence, the soft caresses Jack gave as if he wanted to treasure her.

Equally, she tried to take in all the parts of him. Markings, a tattoo with the Full Throttle gang symbol that covered a pretty wicked scar. She even traced the part of his upper thigh where cybernetic metal met flesh.

"Does this hurt?" The singed flesh where the metal had fused was still rough and bumpy.

Jack shook his head. "No. The surgery couldn't erase the damage left behind from my original injury."

The shower was almost finished, the tell-tale green light beeping above the activator that all contaminates had been removed. He kept touching her though, and she let him, relishing in his worship of her that would end all too soon.

Then she saw it, a small symbol above his left pectoral, the curved markers, the loop and swirl. "This looks strangely familiar."

"It does?" Jack froze, his hands no longer moving. The ion shower turned off. "We better get going. Sun's up and we don't want to test Old Beard's word. Gotta have the hauler to get back to Full Throttle."

She frowned and stepped back. "Yeah, after we get your cure."

The connection between them was severed by some invisible knife Jack had slashed between them, nice and neat. *No way is he gonna get out of this conversation that easily.*

By the time she'd come out of the shower, Jack had exited the bathroom. He was gargling mouth cleaner, judging from the sounds drifting toward her.

"Could you toss me my bag?"

Her black duffle flew through the door and plopped at her feet with a thud. Damn good precision he had, for a driver. She dressed quickly, freshened up, ran some lotion through her curls to keep them from frizzing out in the Mars air. The shower had actually straightened them some, detangling them naturally.

She'd miss this place, the same way she tended to miss her adoptive home. There were some creature comforts she'd never have, always living on the run.

That's what you get for dealing with terrorists. Then, as she finished shoving all her dirty clothes back in the bag and stood up straight she saw it. The symbol on Jack's pec staring right back at her from her own necklace.

What the hell?

* * * *

Almost there. *Damn.*

They'd passed the last marker, letting her know Zephyr was close. All day, they'd traveled since they left the Trading Post, only stopping a couple times for a quick drink, a protein cube or two and bodily relief.

Jack hadn't been up for much talking. No, he napped. Shannon wanted a nap too, but she was the one who knew how to get to Zephyr.

Though she appreciated the silence instead of trying to continue the awkward conversation about her past, even if she wanted to confront him about his tattoo and the relation it had to the necklace she wore. There was something going on here Jack wasn't saying and it reminded her of another memory back at the Full Throttle Watering Hole. When her necklace had been exposed and Jack had seen it dangling from her throat. He'd frozen, suddenly acting a bit different.

Shit.

There was the tell-tale totem, the pole with the bird skull and the spread of feathers painted in human blood. They were the Zephyr symbols that marked the gang-town territory. Because the Auster gangs hadn't built towns like those in Wespero or Aurora, they found it easier to mark their boundaries in certain ways. Zephyr used the poles, believing the painted wood, the skulls and markings would intimidate others encroaching on their territory.

Shannon had always doubted their effectiveness until now. Her stomach twisted in knots with each minute that passed and they moved closer to her past, to a place filled with people who'd made sure she knew exactly what they thought of her. While she'd at first been angry to be traded away, she'd learned fast that being sent to the moon was the best possible future she could have gained.

Coming back now, she regretted not having more to show for her time away.

"Hey, Jack...wake up. We're almost there." *And we need to talk.*

She had to tell him how this would go down, prepare him.

Out of the corner of her eye, she caught his movements. The subtle stretch of his arm, rotation of his neck and arch of his back. All those motions were familiar to her now, and she found some sense of familiarity to him that they hadn't had more than a day ago.

Plus, you've seen him naked.

"I'm awake. Are we almost there?"

"Yeah, and I wanted to give you a heads up for what happens when we get in there. It might not be as simple as it was at the Trading Post."

He laughed. "That was anything but simple and I'm not unfamiliar with weird rituals in gang-towns. So spit it out."

Maybe it was her own fear manifesting as concern for how Jack might react. She took a deep breath as the few buildings Zephyr had constructed came into view. They were down to minutes. "Fine. We'll be searched, our persons, the hauler. They might even separate us to ensure what we're saying lines up. Ideally, let me do the talking, but if they do split us up…just tell the truth. We're here to talk with Noid about business. If they ask what business, just tap that cybernetic leg of yours."

"You don't think that's sharing too much?"

Shannon shook her head. "Most Zephyrs are body purists. They wouldn't want to alter their bodies themselves. No, they'd rather sell the tech and hope that people fuck themselves up more and it takes out the competition."

She dared a glance, taking her foot off the accelerator as they finally came up on Zephyr. Two guards were already motioning for the hauler to slow down.

Jack pursed his lips and his silence set her on edge. Finally, he spoke. "Fine, I'll follow your lead, but the minute I sense something's off, I'll do things my own way."

Shannon brought the hauler to a stop, taking note of the two guards and the two extras that had just emerged from the hut at the end of the street. This was how Zephyr always operated, with a show of force. There would be at least four more out in the open within the next few minutes.

"Hello, folks. We're here to talk to Noid." Shannon propped her arm up on the side of the hauler door doing her best impression of relaxed she could muster.

The guards themselves shared a couple gazes between them.

Then the one closest to her grunted. "Visitors aren't allowed past top-side."

"He's expecting us." Which she wasn't sure if Noid was or wasn't. She wasn't sure if her communication informing him of her imminent arrival had made it. But she had told him she was going to Frog Lick in their last communication. They were tied to that town forever because of the cybernetic trials and Kascade's end goals.

"Then we'll alert him and he can meet you up here."

"Sounds fine to me. Tell me where to park." Shannon's unease notched up a bit as the second guard motioned to the one she'd been talking to. Their helmets with barely see-through visors failed to hide the concern on their faces.

Instead of a response, they aimed their guns at Jack. "Get out of the hauler, now!"

Jack shook his head. "Remember what I said about when this goes to hell?"

Shit.

Chapter Twelve

Jack held his arms up and looked at Shannon. As soon as he opened the door, he would make a move. These two guards with their visor helmets and rifles wouldn't stand a chance if Jack could get in close. They wore vests over shirts and had sulky expressions that reminded him of men who preferred any other job than the one they were stuck on.

"Well, get out," the idiot on his side of the hauler said.

"Sure, but to do so means lowering my hands. Didn't your superiors ever teach you not to let a man's hands out of your sight?"

Idiot number one chuckled. "Funny shit but your hands won't matter. We suspect anything weird, we shoot. No one gets upset as long as we shot first."

"Real good way to kill business partners," Shannon fired back as she opened the door on her side. Jack followed suit, deciding against an attack. He didn't want to risk Shannon's safety if these spaceholes really didn't care about firing their weapons.

Hell, he shouldn't have listened to Shannon in the first place. No way were they getting in here nice and easy. Not when the guard saw his leg and freaked out.

"See...like I said, Kurt. He's not natural." He pointed to the hole in Jack's pants at the knee. Jack should have patched the damn things up a long time ago. The shiny metal of his cybernetic leg was visible.

"Shit, what's something like that doing here?"

Shannon popped off before Jack could respond. "Like I said, to visit Noid. You know he worked with the moonies before coming back home. Has experience with implants and the like."

"Yenna won't like it. She's big on keeping that sort of thing—"

"Why don't you both take a load off? These two are with me." Another voice entered the ring, this from a man who stood shorter than almost everyone present. He barely reached over five foot six, wore a rag wrapped around his head and had pockmarks all over his skin, something Jack recalled was caused by an illness that killed plenty of children.

"Noid, Yenna said no—"

"And I'll keep them top-side for our entire transaction. You let me deal with Yenna."

So, this was Noid, with nuggets bigger than most. He walked toward them, more a sideways strut and that was when Jack noticed his left leg wasn't quite the proper position either, the foot pointed away from him sideways.

The guards left, moving over to another small group that had gathered. The four to six huts were a smokescreen, designed to make people think this town was nothing, with no one. Underneath the dirt, though… Jack flexed his feet a bit, but everything felt solid.

"You're curious, huh?"

"What?" Jack snapped his attention to Noid, who was standing in front of the hauler and grinning at him.

"You're like everyone else, wondering what's down below. Afraid this trip finding out is not part of the plan." Noid gave him a wink then looked at Shannon. "Thought you were done with lost causes. You always said connections are for the weak, but here you are with him."

Jack heard the words and established this wasn't just someone she randomly knew. No, these two had a history and Jack despised the flair of jealousy that radiated through him at the idea this Noid might have gotten to know Shannon better or even intimately.

"Stuff it, Noid. Just get to work."

Noid pulled a handheld device out of the inside of his long coat. "Lemme guess, nanotechnology degradation."

Jack frowned. "How did you know?"

"I predicted it." Noid approached him as his fingers flew across a small keyboard. "Hold still, hands at your side."

Jack did as commanded, tensing and hoping this wasn't a trick to immobilize him. They could take him for experimentation. Even if Shannon said Zephyrs didn't care for those with enhancements, it wouldn't stop them from cutting off his cybernetic leg and selling it to the highest bidder.

"And don't make fists or tense your frame." Noid angled the device and the small green laser light mapped Jack's body. "Relax."

"Easy for you to say," Jack replied. He was already running on a bit of an adrenaline rush from the guards putting them on edge. Now a weird scan with no explanations. This was the stuff that could fuel his nightmares.

"Yeah, I'm not the one suffering. I get it." Noid pressed a button and the device beeped, before a body-wide net, starting at his head, moved downward until it got to Jack's feet then back again. "It's like you thought, degradation. But you were right to come here. I've been working on the solution. Second-gen nanites. Won't break down over time or even with exposure."

"Exposure? What the hell wasn't I supposed to have been doing?" Jack couldn't help the frustration in his voice.

Shannon leaned against the hauler, arms crossed, and Jack's anger rose.

Noid shook his head. "We didn't know right away either, but the program got canceled because long-term exposure to ship engines degrades the nanites. You got lucky, Frog Lick losing their shipbuilding license when they did. Might have given all of you cyborgs a few more years."

"You knew about this?" Jack asked Shannon, even when he already knew the truth.

"Nothing I would have said would have made a difference, at least until now. Knowing Noid had the cure…"

Jack shook his head. "Unbelievable. So, tell me, Noid…how do I save myself and my brothers?"

"It's a simple injection. Once we finish the transfusion, you let the nanites take hold in your system over a week, then you can extract and replicate enough for another injection. Easy-peasy." Noid tucked his scanner back into his coat.

"And we trade you the tech we brought in return." Jack decided not to wait for Noid to name the price. Jack would figure this out himself, even as he fought the ongoing frustration that the two people standing here knew more about the inner workings of the enhancements in his body than he did.

Noid made a little noise with his mouth, glanced at Shannon and shrugged. "I'll be honest, maybe before that would have worked fine. But I'm risking a lot of Yenna's wrath for not letting those guards boot you to begin with. Afraid it's going to cost a bit more."

"You can't even cut us a break for knowing each other." Shannon's half-hearted attempt at a friendly voice got Noid laughing.

"You really tried to make that sound meaningful, but we both know you never cared about anyone but yourself."

Jack didn't like the way those words snaked along his skin, soaking into him fears he'd harbored his whole life. The woman who wore his necklace needed to be a partner.

"Though this cyborg may be a close second contender, what with you bringing him all the way here. I'll tell you what. You run a little gig for me and I think we can work something out."

Shannon shook her head and sat back down in the hauler. "Nope. You can't accept the tech, we're out. You think we're desperate, but he's got time. So do the others, like you said."

"Wait." Jack refused to let this chance to save everyone he cared about walk away without understanding the ask. "What's the job?"

So far Noid hadn't seemed like the manipulative type. No, he was straight-forward and said what needed to be said. Simple tech wouldn't appeal to him and Jack should have realized it from the start. They needed to offer more.

"I'm working on a project and it requires a rare stone. One of the local gang-towns has one, won off a bet with an Upper who was supposed to be bringing the stone to me to sell. Now the gang isn't willing to trade, even though it's worth more to me and I offered a good deal."

Jack nodded. "Yeah, that's rough, but breaking and entering isn't my type of gig."

No, he did racing and muscle. If it were a simple bet or a collection, he could probably handle it. Subterfuge, sneaking around, not really his area of expertise.

Noid pointed at Shannon. "But it's her kind of gig."

No wonder this had become the vocal point of what he wanted because Shannon was here. The woman in question gripped the steering wheel of the hauler so tight her knuckles were white. She stared Noid down with a narrow gaze.

"Shannon?"

She looked at Jack and her expression changed, lightened. He couldn't help but recall their early morning together, chasing oblivion. This woman inspired something crazy in him. "I'm not really into those sorts of jobs anymore."

The honesty in those words… He believed her. Judging how she didn't try to change the subject or laugh the conversation away.

"Yeah, but I'm willing to give it a go, if you have a plan." Jack found himself saying words he would have never considered before. All because a woman looked at him.

"No." Shannon pushed herself out of the seat and back onto the ground, stalking around the back of the hauler and coming up beside him. "I've got this."

"How?" Jack found himself reaching for her hand, as subtly as he could, but she refused to connect with him.

"I wasn't always a nurse, Jack."

Noid chuckled. "No, she wasn't. The pair of us did plenty of questionable things when we were with Humans First."

Humans First—the name curdled in Jack's stomach and once more he was reminded how no matter his feelings for this woman, her background was filled with the kinds of nightmares that might keep haunting her for years to come. He hadn't been part of the terrorist organization, but he'd agreed to them putting this cybernetic limb on him. The goals of the group had been a little mysterious at that time and he'd been desperate to walk again with two legs.

"You were both members?"

Shannon bowed her head a bit, glancing at her feet. "We were. Our expertise and skills in various areas helped get us in the door, but we were often tasked with special missions that may have been less than legal."

"Yeah," Noid continued, "but we were good at it. Though this isn't something that requires my high-tech abilities. There is a safe, but old-Earth-style locking mechanism with a tumbler and everything."

The conversation still sat uneasy with Jack, unsure of how he felt knowing Shannon's past. He wanted to ask more questions without an audience.

"I'm not comfortable with them, but familiar." Shannon looked up and squared her frame. "I assume we're not doing this tonight. We'll need time to plan, to travel."

Noid nodded in agreement. "Sure, have a night to go through things. I'll drop off a holo-tablet to the hut on the end there. You can park your hauler right next to it. Door to the under will be locked. But you're welcome to crash inside. We can reconvene tomorrow afternoon."

"All right. We meet up then." Shannon pointed a finger in Noid's direction. "But, if I don't like it or something seems fishy, we back out and you still give us the second gen."

Noid chuckled as he wrapped the edges of his coat around his body. "You know that's not how this will work, Shannon. Besides, what happened to taking risks, living on your own terms? Last I checked you were still living life the same way… Don't stop now."

Risks… Jack didn't like them, especially when taking one meant playing with his life.

Chapter Thirteen

The hut was like the one from Shannon's childhood—minimally adorned with a wooden table, two chairs, a low-set bed in the corner that could maybe fit two. The mattress was a thin piece of stuffed fabric and no blankets.

"Looks like we're cuddling tonight." Shannon motioned toward the bed then sighed. "Sorry I couldn't get us better accommodations."

Jack hauled their duffels in through the door and tossed them down. The wood creaked in response. "I'm not complaining. We also have enough food and water left from the Argest post, shouldn't need to ask for anything. I'll grab the supply box and then we can settle."

He was distant in his tone of voice, his mannerisms. Nothing like a man who'd seen her naked and brought her to a satisfying climax repeatedly…almost as if he'd been let down by something.

Of course, Shannon could hypothesize all she wanted, but ultimately they needed to talk about this. The very thing she never wanted to talk about—her past. A solid knock rapped against the trap door in the floorboard at the back left corner of the hut. Then the door swung open and a holo-tablet was set on the floor.

"All the info is there," a voice announced. The person who owned it was hidden in shadow, but the hoarse guttural sound meant it wasn't Noid.

"Thanks."

The hinge creaked as the trap door shut, right as Jack walked back in. Shannon marched over and picked up the tablet, thumbing through the details for a quick skim.

"What's that?" he asked as he set their small crate of supplies on the table.

"The details for our heist. At a glance, shouldn't be an issue, but I might need your help as a lookout." Shannon would need his help and possibly Noid's. No way could she just walk in and get away with this without a distraction in place. There was time to figure that out before they left tomorrow.

"I can definitely play the role of eyes, no problem." He opened the canister of water and took a good swallow before holding it out to her.

She set the holo-tablet on the table and took the container from him. "This might be more involved than that."

The water cooled her throat, helping ease a little bit of the nervous energy coursing through her at the coming conversation. How she'd need to dredge up her past in ways she'd hadn't spoken of to anyone in years...not since she'd spilled her heart to Kascade and in turn he'd abused her past for his own gain.

"How so? I mean, I'm not a fan of the idea, especially since if you fail, I don't get what I need."

She set down the canister and sealed it back up. "That's why I won't fail, because there isn't an option for us to leave empty handed. If we do, I don't get paid."

Pulling out a chair, she sat down at the table and let out a sigh. "I get you're not comfortable with this—you can't control the outcome—but I would have figured you'd learned by now that I don't bet if I can't win."

Jack grabbed the other chair and started pulling items out of the supply box. "Oh, no, I acknowledge you're confident in your abilities. I won't lie, though. You like to hide things and it makes me worried you're hiding other stuff."

"Like?" She wasn't going to throw more out in the open than she needed to.

"How'd you get familiar with breaking and entering?"

She reached for the container of protein cubes and decided then and there to be honest. *Maybe it'd wise him up, keep him from probing for more.* Maybe she'd get a good reminder why being on her own was better than trusting any part of her future to someone else. "I used to spend hours locked in a room. Sometimes days if I was unlucky. The only way to escape was to learn how."

"Why were you locked up?" Jack's sympathy kept her from looking at him.

No, I have to be emotionless.

"Because I was a murderer."

Jack barked out a laugh. "I find that awful hard to believe."

She snapped her head up and narrowed her eyes at him. "Really? You think I couldn't?"

"Oh, anyone is capable in the right circumstances, but you were a kid."

"I killed my mother coming out of her. You think having an enhanced body is a bad thing. It's not the only superstition these damn Zephyrs use as a way to build themselves up and break others down."

Jack sobered. "I'm sorry. That's a medical travesty, not something you blame a child for."

"In Auster, people aren't as forgiving. I was called a murderer by adults, children…everyone. They wanted nothing to do with me. I was locked away whenever my father felt like it. Then traded away to moonies so I'd at least be worth something.

"Those skills were then enhanced by my adoptive parents. I learned more about technology, human anatomy and how if we'd just had a certain monitor and a particular medication from the Uppers, my mother might have lived giving birth to me. Of course, my eagerness to see all people on equal footing is what lured me to Kascade's Humans First group. That's where Noid and I became friends, where the prejudices from childhood were washed away from years of being nowhere near this place. Except, when Humans First imploded, Noid was welcomed back. I, on the other hand, still have nowhere to go."

Somehow, she felt relieved to say all of that, to spew it out and get it off her chest. Even if Jack rebuked her or made fun of her story, at least she'd come out with it.

Of course you left out the most important stuff.

"Homeless, but not without skill and talent. It's got to be worth something. Your abilities were worth Full Throttle signing you on."

Shannon shrugged and tried not to get frustrated with how easy Jack was taking this. "Sure, but it's nothing permanent."

"Only because you haven't asked if it could be." He dead-stared her for a good five seconds and her chest grew tight. She couldn't breathe.

"My turn to tell you a story."

She waited as he ate a food cube and took another drink. She flexed her fists and pursed her lips to keep from shouting for him to hurry up.

"I told you about my mother gambling away our belongings, but in particular...I made her a necklace for her birthday one year. Something to try and cheer her up. I carved our family symbol out of an animal bone. See, my father married my mother and took her name, as a homage to her father and to carry on the family name that would have died out. He truly gave her everything... Anyway, she gambled the damn necklace away on a game of chance. Risking a gift for a single shot of shine."

Jack's fist thudded against the table. "Maybe if she'd been parting with it to buy food for us or even clothing, something of worth... I could have forgiven that."

Shannon's heart clenched at how heartbroken Jack sounded. How this one act had destroyed whatever good feelings he had for the woman who'd birthed him. Similar to how she'd lost her love for the father who hated her. She reached up and pulled the carved bone out from underneath her shirt, and clenched it tight in her palm.

"My father refused to let me hate her or the others in Frog Lick who kept encouraging her. No, he said, it was fate. Fate that took the necklace away, that my carving would go out into the world and find someone special and when it was time..." Jack looked at her again, first her eyes, then at her throat where she kept the carving safe. "The necklace would return to me with the person I was supposed to be with. My mother was doing me a favor. I've held onto that story for so long, wondering for years where my necklace ended up."

Shannon let the carving fall out of her hand, swinging wide as the rope pulled tight against her neck from the weight. "I found it."

"You saw then?"

She nodded. "Your tattoo on your arm. I recognized it somewhere and then it dawned on me, the necklace. I've had this since I got to the moon. It was the first thing I was allowed to have that was mine. Something I chose."

Those words hung heavy in the air between them. She had an urge to move toward him, to close the distance. This entire time, she'd been tied to Jack, and he to her, if his father's story held any bit of truth.

"It doesn't have to mean anything, but it seems pretty impossible that a necklace lost to an off-worlder would have come back to Mars, to my town specifically."

Shannon decided to go with action over words. She shoved her chair out of the way and went to Jack, going in for the kiss, letting her tongue and lips do the talking. The idea they were somehow bound, somehow made whole because of this charm she wore around her neck was ridiculous and yet... *Why does it feel so damn right?*

Her hands roamed, across his wide shoulders, gripping his biceps, the muscle there. The exploration continued and he joined in as well. What started as a mutual, slow connection turned into a fast-paced race for who could get their clothes off first.

They broke apart and she watched with delight as Jack removed his shirt, boots, pants. Everything was gone and she matched his enthusiasm with a strip show of her own. Soon they were both naked and panting, with mere inches separating them.

"That bed could break." Jack cocked his head toward their mattress only a foot or so off the ground.

"I'm willing to give those who might be listening a show."

Jack laughed and reached for her, pulling her flush against his body. She sighed in relief as their bare skin met, his belly to hers, his hard cock pulsing between them.

"You're crazy."

"And you love it. Now, fuck me."

He picked her up, like she weighed nothing, cradling her against him. Their lips met and Shannon let herself get lost in how he kissed, with such want and desire. He acted like he wanted to eat her up, the way he nipped and sucked on her lower lip.

Lowering them both to the mattress, the groan he let loose alarmed her and she pulled back from the embrace. "Are you okay?"

"My leg."

Enough said. She pushed on his pecs. "Let me go. I'll stand and you lie down."

"But—" There was frustration in his eyes, the way he gripped her tighter as if determined to prove his body wrong.

"You're no good to me broken. I need you for the heist tomorrow."

He growled. "Fine."

She only fell about a foot when he let her go and she did her best not to make a sound. No sense in adding to the already present guilt he carried. *I'll make him feel good.*

Scrambling out of his way, she let Jack lie down before putting her hands on him, all over him. She massaged the tissue of his upper thigh where flesh met metal, using her other hand to start stroking him.

"You don't have to touch me there. It's not pretty." His eyes were shut tight, as if he feared to see her reaction.

She let go of his cock and leaned down to press a kiss to the scarred flesh, where he'd been burned and injured. "Every part of you is gorgeous. It's what makes you unique. Don't dismiss this difference as something not worthy of admiration or affection."

He opened his eyes then and the emotion present sat heavy in her chest. "No one has ever said that to me. They just ignore that part of my anatomy."

"Well, let me be the first to say I like to celebrate differences. They speak to our experiences, the risks we took to get where we are." She started to stroke him again, this time with a little more speed. "And I personally would also like to celebrate this delicious dick of yours. So long, so hard and perfect for my mouth."

Jack had wanted to say something to Shannon, but those words died as soon as she wrapped her mouth around him. His eyes rolled and he clenched the side of the poorly stuffed mattress with both hands, determined to let Shannon drive the pace of this encounter.

Emotionally, he was all over the place, unsure of what to expect from the future and desperate to be present in the now, this moment where Shannon desired him, even the less attractive bits. Where she was momentarily honest about where she'd come from and how they both shared childhoods that weren't the greatest.

All those thoughts fled, though, as she snaked a hand up to cup his balls, gently massaging, until a couple of fingers worked their way backward.

"What are you doing?"

She popped off his dick and gave a smile. "A little trick I picked up. Are you okay with me trying something new?"

He nodded. "Go ahead."

Submitting to her was easy and instead of being turned off by her experimental, risk-prone antics, he found himself eagerly wanting to chase after her. To see what came next.

She found a place under his balls, back toward his anus, and massaged. He jerked in response at first.

"Relax and let me make you feel good," she replied, the words murmured as she rubbed her lips against the head of his cock, controlling the motions with her other hand.

Whatever she did, it was working. He started to get the feeling he'd pop off at the slightest provocation. A tingling sensation coupled with the need to pump had him doing his best not to buck under her.

"You want to thrust, huh?" She looked up at him with a grin. "Then thrust. Fuck my mouth like you're inside me. Don't worry, I've got you."

She swallowed him up again and he tentatively moved. He was shocked by her urging. The request was unlike any he'd heard. Once again, he felt guilty for not giving more pleasure to her and seemingly taking all for himself.

She moaned, and her vocalization vibrated against his cock. Paired with the stimulation she was administering underneath his balls, he couldn't stop himself.

Slow, measured movements became surges upward, drawn into the sweet, suction motions of her mouth. Heaven wouldn't be this amazing. Then he pumped in earnest, desperate to reach the peak she'd helped him climb. He wanted to come, to find the finish line like a driver behind a racer, foot pounding the accelerator.

Whatever he dished out, she took, enthusiastically urging him on by continuing her massage of his flesh. Until he was at the breaking point.

"I'm going to—"

The orgasm hit him hard, causing his thighs to spasm and his back to arch as he shot his load. Shannon didn't pull away—she swallowed every bit. When she finally sat up, licking her lips and smiling wide, Jack was stunned to silence. This woman was a sensual being of the most perverse sense and he loved this aspect of her.

Shocking him to his core, the dual hit to his senses rattled his emotional and physical centers. He'd believed he knew what he wanted before and Shannon had whittled away at those ideas with each day they had spent together. Physically, mentally, she should have been the last thing he wanted. Instead, he was starting to think he might be unable to be without her before this was done.

She sat up and smiled, having effectively swallowed the evidence of his pleasure. "You're delicious. Too bad we aren't back at the Trading Post."

"Why?" He found himself unable to hypothesize a reason, not so soon after coming and still reeling from his own realizations.

Shannon crawled up his body slowly, dragging her tits across his stomach and chest. How did she make even these movements feel so erotic? He twitched beneath her at the feel of them skin on skin, his nerve endings still so sensitive from her milking him to completion.

"Because then I'd let you get me all messy. I'd squirt everywhere." She was face-to-face with him. Leaning down, she kissed him and he tasted his salty essence on her lips.

What a fucking rush.

"Is that what you call what happened this morning?"

She nodded. "It's a form of release that I don't share with many. Men and women I've been with in the past weren't exactly aroused by my body's response."

"I enjoyed it. If you want to do that again, right now...sit on my face." Jack was almost shocked at how bold he talked with her. Usually he wooed women, kept his words flowery, but with Shannon, all sense of censoring himself fled.

Shannon pressed a hand to her chest right above her breasts as if shocked, but her smile said the opposite. "You sure know the way to win a woman's heart. Are you going to lick my pussy?"

"I'm going to feast on you until you blast my face."

She grinned and nodded. "I'm down for that."

Jack hauled her the rest of the way up his body, hooking his arms under her legs to spread her wide and get that wet center of hers where he needed it—his mouth.

"Better hold on. I'm not stopping until you explode."

Chapter Fourteen

"Give me two," Jack said, tossing a couple of low cards from his hand and waiting for the dealer, their host, to give him replacements.

Last night was like a fever dream compared to now, sitting at a table with five other men he didn't know. They were in the gang-town of Skeiron. Shannon had almost cursed when she took a second look at the holotablet this morning.

"It's not a woman-friendly gang. They keep their females under lock and key. I've never seen one on the surface. Hell, for all we know, they don't have any."

The Skeiron gang-town had been in the final race one time since Jack was old enough to remember. They were an all-male crew with lean wiry bodies and sharpened teeth. Wespero gangs jokingly called Skeiron vultures, circling others waiting to pick off the scraps from the dead.

"You sure you're in?" asked the host, Wotan, a man with long black hair from the center of his head like a shaggy mohawk. He'd been shaved bald on either side. When he grinned with those pointed teeth designed to rip and tear, Jack had to lock his shoulders so he wouldn't shudder.

Jack had asked Shannon the same question that morning, but instead of fearing whatever would come of robbing Skeiron, she'd gotten a little excited. Almost too eager to stick it to those patriarchal bastards, as she'd put it.

He tossed another slip of crinkle to the center. "Yeah, I'll call."

Wotan and the others tapped the table in unison. One by one, they laid down their cards. There were little chuckles of mirth as each set of five was better than the last. Two pair, three jacks, a hand of hearts and finally…

"My turn." Jack gave his best sheepish shrug. "Maybe I should've taken the warning when I arrived."

He flipped his cards over and leaned back in the seat for the effect his full house, two aces and three fives, elicited with multiple groans. There was a sharp scrape of wooden chairs as two of the players stood. He recalled their names vaguely. Wotan stared him down, grinning the entire time.

"You're more than we expected. Most who walk through those doors with an introduction from Noid don't typically deliver on the pitch. You actually know how to play cards."

Unfortunately.

"I'm surprised you let me in if Noid's reputation is he brings you space fish and klogs."

Wotan gave a nod toward Jack's legs under the table. "You walk different, heavy sound. Imagined you might be worth getting to know regardless of how you played."

"Flip your cards." Jack had to keep the game going, until he received the signal from Shannon that her thievery was complete.

"Sure, but remember...we're really good at cards too." Wotan revealed a straight, a lovely sequence of low cards in order and shine on the metal... They were the same suit.

Skeiron were cheaters. No doubt about it. Jack would need to pull deep into his repertoire of a past life he'd despised to get through this evening.

I shouldn't have agreed to this.

One of the others lit a fat chunk then, the distinct smell of marijuana coated in something far less innocent drifting through the room. There was shine in tall bottles, something called rye whiskey in some. These men were surrounding themselves in all the vices that came from Earth. Even Wotan took to sniffing cocaine directly from a pouch he kept on his wrist.

"You won that one."

Wotan dipped into his pouch with a finger, coating it in white powder before rubbing the drug all over his gums. A drop of red appeared on his fingertip from where he'd pricked it against his teeth. "Whoops." He sucked it into his mouth. "These games are getting exciting. It's your deal next."

His deal...the cards, the drinking, the casual drug use. He took a deep breath and almost choked on the scent of the laced marijuana. This all reminded him of the parties in the Watering Hole before Drag had taken over and they'd decided to make Frog Lick less about getting lost in vice and more focused toward a common goal.

Shannon, hurry the hell up.

Because he was already agitated. His skin crawled with the desperate need for fresh air, escape, anything to get away from these people who reminded him of the ones that would steal from his mother. They'd play and play with the promise that one more game might change her luck. One more flip of a card could have her gaining back everything she'd already lost.

Gathering the cards, he started to shuffle, numbing himself to the sounds of laughter, the shared mirth that these men seemed to have in their intoxicated state.

"Sure you don't want any?" This was from the red-haired man next to him, shoving the chunk toward him.

Jack shook his head, keeping his expression neutral and focusing on the cards in his hands. "I'm good. Once this is over, I'll have to drive back to my rooms."

Wotan snorted. "Staying with those Zephyrs? Surprised they'd take you in. They don't like outsiders."

"I don't imagine any gang does." Jack separated the deck and angled the cards to flip them back together. "Only for a night, though, then I make my way."

"To the next card game?" the redhead asked as he took another big toke off the chunk.

Besides the four people at the table, there were others engaged in various games of their own. Dice on one table, knives on another, a wheel with a round rock. Noid had told Jack he'd introduce him to the person he needed to keep occupied.

"Always up for a good game."

Wotan motioned around them. "Then you see Skeiron is good for exactly that. Games, we have tons of them."

The cards had been sufficiently shuffled and Jack shoved the deck over to the redhead to cut. "Afraid I prefer cards."

Because that was what his mother had taught him. After so many times of being beaten, she'd not only taken Jack with her to play lookout for suspicious behavior, she'd taught him every possible game folks would try with fifty-two little squares. Maybe she'd wanted to get better or just ensure Jack didn't fall in all the ways she'd had. But...he'd still suffered.

"A real bumdum, because we like playing all types." Red-Hair cut, then pushed the deck back to Jack.

He did what was expected, but his eyes bothered him. He had a desire for something to drink besides the shine swill. How much longer? "Five card right or how about we change things up?"

"Change things?" Red-Hair repeated.

"Yeah, you like games. I know lots of them with cards. We could seven card hold this one."

Wotan cocked his head. "Seven card hold? We don't get an extra exchange?"

Jack started to deal. "Nope, seven cards, you make the best five of whatever you get. No exchanges."

Everyone had already thrown their flash in for the ante.

"Sounds like we don't get options to improve," another said.

Jack stopped at five cards, in case they didn't agree. "But you get two extras. Agree now or play it safe... Funny, I was told Skeirons liked to take the most risk. Maybe not."

"Deal the extra cards, Jack Renfro." Wotan spoke his words like a command, a scowl on his face. He'd deliberately used Jack's last name as well. A reminder they knew who he was. But Jack wasn't intimidated by small threats.

The last two cards were out, and he set the deck down. Before any of the cards were picked up, Red-Hair threw in two strips of crinkle.

"You say you like risk—then let's raise the ante before anyone looks."

Jack gave a nod of agreement, even as he lamented his ever-dwindling clump of flash. He had to make this last. According to Noid, it was the biggest amount the ex-terrorist had access to. But when playing with cheaters, even an endless pot didn't guarantee wins. *Though in this game it will be more difficult for them to cheat.*

Wotan shook his head and shoved the cards across the table. "Changed my mind. I don't like this game. Think I'll take a break, maybe come back after I check a few things."

Fuck.

Their target was going to leave the table and Shannon hadn't signaled. Red-Hair chortled between drags of his chunk.

Another player nearly spat whiskey across the table. "Wotan, really?"

Their leader with his shaggy mane of black-as-a-tire hair shook his head. "Play on. I need a minute."

Jack had to do something fast. "Didn't take you for someone who scared so easily, Wotan. You're supposed to lead this gang, right?"

The chair Wotan sat in went flying across the room with barely a shove from Wotan's hand. The conversations around them ceased.

"You calling me a scurdy?"

I'm in it now. Leg, hold up on me.

"And if I am?" Jack shoved out of his chair and stood, then gave the wooden piece a firm kick with his cybernetic leg. The damn thing flew straight into the front door and broke apart. If they wanted a show of strength, he'd give them one.

He had to do what he needed to. At least this ridiculous gambling would stop. Maybe all the rest of the debauchery as well.

"You stand by those words, then there's no stopping what comes next."

Jack grinned and flexed his fists. It'd been a while since he'd gotten in a knockdown, throwdown. He preferred to not fight, becoming even more passive since Drag had taken over. Peace, calmness... *Fuck it.*

"Then go ahead and bring it, but remember you were the one who left the table first."

* * * *

Breaking the lock on the steel doors at the back of the Skeiron game hall wasn't difficult at all. Noid left her there with nothing but a single torch that could attach to her wrist and a two-shot pistol designed for children, not her.

"This is all you have?"

Noid shrugged. "Best I got on short notice. Now enough, those Skeirons are ruthless. I'll be shocked if your man lasts more than thirty solar minutes in there."

"He's not my man," she replied as she adjusted the torch and pocketed the gun.

"Yenna's spies might say otherwise."

Her cheeks heated at the memories of the previous night, how she'd brought Jack to orgasm a couple times and he'd returned the favor. Sure, she'd been full of bravado in the moment, not caring who heard them, but after being confronted with the knowledge, it bothered her.

She flipped Noid off and carefully stepped into the welcoming darkness. How long since she'd been underground on her home planet? Over fifteen years. The moonie bases were nothing like the Auster tunneled cities. Moonie bases still had views to the outside, occasional sunlight and opportunities to spacewalk.

To go to ground in Auster meant being submerged in complete darkness from time to time and a slim chance a person didn't come back. There were stories of collapsed passages and rooms due to improper support. She had no idea what she was venturing into. The stairs downward turned and went deeper. The air was humid and stank of marijuana.

A pink hazy glow drifted up toward her from the bottom. She was almost there but far further than she'd expected. Noid's outline hadn't mentioned two flights of stairs and without a clear-cut path to the top, she ran the risk of not hearing the warning if someone came.

"I'll bang on the doors." Noid had considered this his best option.

"Idiot should have brought communicators." But most likely he didn't have them. Living on Mars again had proven how her time with the moonies had made her too comfortable with technology and accustomed to having access to almost anything she wanted. Here on this arid planet, a person would be lucky for the bare minimum.

The floor plan opened up at the bottom, exactly as the map had displayed—a medium-sized room to the left was covered with plastic sheeting…and the pink light, the rows of rack and herb.

They're doing things they aren't supposed to.

The marijuana growing was evidence enough of illegal enterprise. Drugs and booze were Earth's domain, left to the families of dealers that operated there. The runners and bootleggers were contracted to transport such vices to other planets, moons and anywhere people occupied in between.

I'll tell Noid.

He could do more damage with the information. The rest of the room was the office, several bookshelves, a couple chests filled with who knew. A desk, a holo-tablet and computing system. The Skeiron weren't poor or as disconnected as everyone thought. They were just hiding their capabilities.

Wonder what else they are hiding?

Shannon moved toward the desk, then the wall behind it. A painting hung there, a slither elegantly crafted onto the surface. The two beady eyes stared at her along with a mouth filled with sharp teeth. The Skeiron revered the damn slithers, admired them. They even sharpened their teeth to fine points in worship. Even more like the slithers, Skeiron preferred to operate in darkness, not daylight.

Makes me sick.

The eyes were weird though, and Shannon pressed them. A click sounded in the wall and the section of the slither's face fell forward on a hinge, revealing the door to the safe. The rotating combination wheel was right there.

Winner, winner.

She wanted to celebrate this moment with someone…no, with Jack. Jack who'd brought her to completion and let her soak his face. Yesterday sat on her list of top ten days. A bit disconcerting that spending her day in two different sexual encounters with a man who didn't need her long term could be one of her best.

They were similar in so many ways, with a general distaste for the world they'd grown up in. And the necklace. She instinctively reached for it, rubbing the charm underneath her shirt.

"All right, safe, time to get you unlocked." She started in on the combination, twirling the wheel, listening for the tell-tale clicks to reveal the numbers that would have the door swing open. She didn't need long. No, this one had a simple combination of only single numbers.

"Dumb." The Skeiron who'd set it had obviously been fearful of forgetting.

The door swung open, revealing all the treasures inside. There were several bags of flash, heavy and full, papers, several canisters of seeds and dead center a giant pink stone. The thing was easily as big as her palm.

She grabbed it, resisting the temptation to take the flash. *My, I could run. Get my own ship.*

But then the Skeirons would be after them for far more. No sense in bringing another problem on their heads. Even if she loved sticking it to these Skeiron idiots who didn't believe in feminine value.

Making quick work of hiding the stone in her belt pouch, she closed the safe back up, and replaced its fake door. *Slithers…ugh.*

With no time to waste, she ignored all the other things she could have explored, the chemist set, the medical equipment and the glass case of two or three adolescent slithers. *What the fuck?*

She slowed at that, needing to know more, when a sudden metal bang, single and solid, echoed from the stairwell. *Noid's warning.*

Running up the stairs, she got to the top and braced herself against the wall to catch her breath.

"Did you get it?" Noid asked, his eyes wild as he glanced around.

"Are we discovered?"

Noid shook his head. "Not exactly."

"What's that mean? Where's Jack?" She forked over the stone, which put a big smile on Noid's face as soon as the pink glimmery rock was in his hands. "Noid, answer me."

She set to putting the metal doors back in place as quietly as she could. No way to fix the lock—that would be the giveaway something else went down.

"We're safe, but Jack may have started a bar fight to keep us that way."

Shannon stood, clenched her fists and pivoted to charge for the front door of the gaming hall. "Then we have to help him."

Noid shook his head and pocketed the stone. He let out a good whistle and a hauler emerged from the dark. Not the one they'd arrived in, but one of the Zephyr's. The driver was one of the guards she'd seen last night.

"Afraid this is where I cut and run. We're going to get going before they can suspect anything else."

"The guy you brought to the place just started a brawl and you think it won't lead back to you." She crossed her arms, debating if she should try to take Noid down, but the big muscle in the front seat already had a taser pointed in her direction. "Jack's nanites are fucking decaying. You made a deal, and we did our part."

She'd throw a rock after they drove off, and once she got Jack out they'd rain down hell on the Zephyrs.

"Yep, you did." Noid reached into his coat pocket and Shannon changed her stance, ready to run, duck or bolt at the first sign of violent intent. Instead, he pulled out a tube filled with a thick gray sludge. "Catch."

The tube went up in the air and she dove for it, exhaling in relief after she caught it.

"All you need is a synthesizer. So, here's hoping you both make it out of here alive."

The hauler pulled away and Shannon couldn't help but yell after him, "If I ever see you again, I'm going to make sure you walk funny with both legs."

Getting up and tucking the tube away in the same pouch she'd kept the gem, Shannon ripped off her sleeve and pressed it around the canister of sludge. *Please be enough to keep it safe.*

She headed for the front door next, pulling her little two-shooter out and leaving the torch on. At this point, she'd give someone an ass sting and maybe blind them, but regardless, she'd go out fighting.

Die the way I want.

Hell, she didn't want to die at all. Not without saving Jack, not without being with him. Shit, these feelings for him were becoming something she didn't want to deal with. They were supposed to be in a mutual partnership. One that didn't involve their emotions, but affection had snuck in anyway.

She blamed it on the mind-blowing delicious sex they'd enjoyed together. That was the reason when she burst through the swinging front doors her heart clenched at the sight of Jack trading blows with some red-haired fool, while another was about to crash a bottle of booze over his head.

Aim. Steady your arm. Train the sight. Fire.

Chapter Fifteen

Jack heard the single shot, but was too busy to attempt to figure out who the gun was aimed at. He prayed it wasn't him because he was too busy blocking blows from Red-Hair to take a different defensive action.

Like I could dodge a bullet.

Seconds passed as he avoided another hit from Red-Hair and moved to deliver a nice right hook. No bullet and no pain. Only the groan of another behind him and a heavy thud against the floorboards.

He didn't get a chance to look. His hook landed, shoving Red-Hair back a couple steps, but the force he'd deployed sent his leg into a spasm. Red-Hair caught his hesitation and bumped his fists together as he came for Jack all over again.

His leg refused to cooperate, even a little. He dropped to one knee and, in that brief moment, he didn't care what happened to him. He only hoped Shannon had found what she needed. If he died, then at least the cure for the nanites could be taken back to Full Throttle.

The punch rocked him backward, the pain in his leg worse from the way his body took the impact. He fell forward then she was there.

Shannon…

She jumped in and flashed a bright light in Red-Hair's eyes before bashing him over the head with a small metal object. When she glanced back at him, concern etched into her features, the relief in his gut meant far more than the fact he couldn't keep his eyes open.

"You're alive."

"Jack!"

He closed his eyes then, his name on her lips the last thing he heard. Whatever happened, she was living and breathing. He expected she'd make a break without him.

* * * *

The world is messy.

World, universe…everything was a mess. Jack swallowed hard, his throat dry. He smacked his lips but didn't want to open his eyes. No, he wanted to keep dreaming of Shannon and him dancing at the Watering Hole. Celebrating the Full Throttle win — the championships were coming and his leg hurt. Damn, his leg hurt.

The agonizing pain spread with each passing second. Jack opened his eyes. A small, heavy tube sat in his lap. He wasn't on the ground anymore. No, he was propped up against the wall right to the left of the door to the Skeiron gaming hall. There were three bodies on the floor.

The other players.

Jack remembered knocking one of them out with the table. Cards, broken bottles, broken chairs, the table split in two and the remnants of Red-Hair's chunk were strewn across the floor around the bodies. They'd made a damn mess.

Where's Shannon?

He could move his head just fine, though his cheek was damn sore, and starting to swell. He reached for the cold rag at the back of his neck. Red-Hair could throw a punch. Voices got him glancing around the room. There were still a few patrons huddled near the bar in the center of the room. No, Shannon.

But he heard her speaking.

Her sarcastic chuckle. "I get another throw. If I win, we get to leave?"

"That's the bet. Don't take too long," Wotan responded, his raspy voice a dead giveaway.

There were boots against the floor then he saw her. She came from his left. Her curls held less bounce, and there was a thin sheen of sweat on her forehead and a drop of blood at the corner of her mouth.

I'll kill them all.

"You're awake." She rushed toward him, dropping to her knees as she ran her hands across his shoulders.

"Yeah...who made you bleed?"

She yanked the cold rag away from his hands and pressed it gently to his hot cheek. "You should be asking what I did to the guy who knocked you out."

He hissed at the initial contact, then covered her hand with his, to feel something, to know this moment was real and he wasn't dreaming any longer. "Who did it?"

"Wotan caught me by surprise, but I convinced him to give me a shot to win our freedom."

Jack snorted. "You would."

She was unbelievable, a true survivor, seeking any means to prolong her life. And, for some dumb reason, she'd decided to try to save him too. He wanted to argue that point and demonstrate how she should have made for the hauler and escaped at all costs.

"They're cheaters."

She winked at him. "Yeah, I'm familiar with that. Why do you think Wotan's getting so impatient? Luckily, I got him to agree to my terms."

"How did you do that?"

She nudged the tube in his lap, filled with a gray sludge. Then leaned in closer to whisper in his ear. "Wotan believes the gray shit in your lap is a bomb. But Noid delivered as soon as I gave him the stone. This is what you need."

The nanites.

Fuck, she really should have left him to die. They weren't risking just his life by trying to get both of them out of here—they were risking his family's.

"And Noid?"

"Long gone," she replied. "Our host still isn't aware of the other bit just yet."

"Hey!" Wotan's aggravated tone filtered over to them. "You got two minutes to get back up here for the last throw. I'm done waiting."

Shannon waved a hand in Wotan's direction. "All right, I'm coming. Just catching my baby up. I told you I don't make a move without his direction."

The cold compress came away from his cheek then and he could finally look at her with both eyes. All this pressure and she still wore a smile, still acted like this wasn't nothing she couldn't get them both through.

"Should have left me. You're risking too much. There are other lives at stake than just mine."

She shushed him, then cupped his cheek before briefly pressing her lips to his. "You're cute when you go all self-sacrifice mode. But afraid I don't want to be on the receiving end of Drag's wrath if I don't return with you."

"You're amazing," he mumbled, even though her actions triggered a riot inside him. On one hand, he appreciated her commitment to saving him, but on the other, he was disheartened that her motivation was still her own survival.

The way her face lit up, the brightened tone in her eyes, was worth his words though. "You're the first person to really think so. I hit the target with this knife and we're out of here. Wotan promised to let us go. A kiss for good luck?"

He nodded. It would take his mind off the sharp sticks of pain emanating from his leg and up into his spine. This was worse than before, but he wouldn't tell her that now. *No, she needs to focus.*

Shannon leaned in and pressed another soft kiss to his lips. But he refused to let her pull back this time. Clutching her head to his, he deepened the connection. He traced the seam of her entrance with his tongue and found a rush of endorphins when she engaged with him in return. Whatever happened next, he'd remember this.

A couple hoots and hollers echoed around them. They had an audience. *Fuck 'em.*

When she pulled back, she lifted the necklace he'd made and pressed a kiss to that as well. "Here goes nothing."

Jack used the time that Shannon took getting back to the knife throw area to resituate so he could see better. He tested the strength of his arms and his remaining human leg. Thankfully, all of those limbs were capable of getting him up.

A glance down at the tube in his lap…hell, salvation for his pain sat in his hands and he was still helpless. They could only pray their hauler hadn't been taken by Noid or discovered by the Skeirons.

"You'd better not be tampering with my knives, Wotan."

The Skeiron leader chuckled. "Tampering… I think you got me all wrong. I like games and your man over there ruined the one we were enjoying. Got all bothered because I was leaving the table."

She shrugged. "He's a purist. Doesn't believe people should exit a table before the game is over."

"Well, he needs to take some lessons from me then. You might do for a few lessons yourself… Why get hung up with that fool over there?"

The sludge sack was flirting with her. *Of course, he is.* Jack's shoulders tensed and he hated the jealousy simmering under his skin. This wasn't going to work. He felt too much for her and she wasn't the type to want to settle, to stay. She'd already said as much—she chased adrenaline. Risks and games of chance, which he couldn't stand. He could see that in the way she lived, too vibrant for settling in Frog Lick.

Too addicted to her own adventure to settle with me.

"Aww, you think I need some teaching. That's rich coming from a man who can't seem to keep a woman."

Wotan grunted in frustration. "We have women. They know their place and stay out of sight. You would do well to learn from them. Throw the knife."

Jack watched on, unable to do anything but send up silent pleas that she'd hit her target. He didn't doubt her. She'd done amazing with the darts and had pretty good aim in general.

She tossed the knife in her hand, flipping it a couple times and catching the handle. Then she balanced the blade on the end of two fingertips. Taking a sharp breath, she exhaled slowly. "All right then. Here's to freedom."

The blade whistled through the air, a sharp sound, almost imperceptible compared to the other low-level noises in the room. Except, she was off, by more than an inch. The blade hit the outside of the target.

Fuck. Time to get crazy.

"Well, seems you messed with my blade after all. It wasn't balanced." Because she didn't miss. Not with knives, darts, cards... Missing wasn't in her vocabulary. She'd spent too many nights training her skills, honing them so she wouldn't find herself at the mercy of anyone ever again, no matter what planet in the universe she traveled to.

She glanced at Jack and smiled. No sense in worrying him. *I go out my way.*

Wotan shrugged. "You didn't say anything. You threw it and you said you were good." The disappointment in his voice was funny. As if he found the spirit of competition so important to lose to a less than worthy opponent he took offense.

"Well, I lost, obviously." Shannon needed a minute, just sixty seconds to determine alternatives. Another game... Wotan didn't respect her, so unlikely. She'd only gotten the opportunity at this one because she'd knocked out two of his gang members.

"So, you lose. Now, we get the bomb. We get you, and your man...he gets a knife to the belly."

"Wait!" She could trade Noid and the stone. Sell his ass out for ditching them. *No...*

"I'm going to detonate if you don't call your guys off." Jack thrust the canister of the nanites up in the air, the release button under his thumb. "One press, five seconds later this whole building is gone. How's that for a game, Wotan?"

Sharp teeth grinned at her. "What's his deal?"

"He'll go out of this universe on his terms, nothing less." Of course, that was her philosophy, but this patriarchal asshole wouldn't respect them from her.

"What if he's bluffing?" Wotan flipped the knife in his hand, he still held one of them. As pointy as his teeth, but far larger.

A couple other gang members had gathered around their leader, ready to launch at the word. She was too far from Jack. He might be able to stand, but he'd need help.

"Is it worth finding out? Risk this gaming hall and your fancy office and contraband hiding beneath?"

Wotan's gaze narrowed and Shannon didn't care that she'd revealed the truth of their arrival. He needed to take them seriously even if they were lying their asses off. Though she believed he would get the seriousness of the issue. All she had to do was send a couple transmissions to Earth—a few interested parties would be here within a solar week to investigate the drugs growing underneath them.

"Fine. I have a terrain uni-rider outside." Wotan pulled a keyring from his belt and tossed it to her. "Take the crazy and go."

She moved toward Jack, not taking her eyes off the gathered gang. There were probably more outfitting themselves underground. "You up?"

"Yeah." The pained response from Jack had her giving him a quick glance. He was standing, not putting any weight on his cybernetic leg.

"Then move toward that uni. I'm coming."

The gang was following them, striding in unison toward her and Jack. For every three steps she took, they did the same. They weren't out of this yet.

Out of the door, down the steps. All backward walking and taking mini-checks on Jack to ensure he didn't fall. Somehow, he made it, but his grunts and growls told her he struggled. Her chest clenched tight at how this fucking bargain they'd struck with Noid might result in them not getting back to Frog Lick. No follow-through, and if something happened to Jack on her watch... *Nope, focus.*

She reached the uni-rider and helped Jack get on.

He held the tube aloft. "Don't come down those steps!"

Wotan and a group of ten men had gathered behind him. They were all flashing those sharp, pointy teeth in grimacing grins, holding various knives, chains...no guns. A good sign.

"Oh, we will...for now." Wotan's words resulted in the rest of the group collectively laughing. "We catch you in our territory again and you're dead."

They had less than two hours to clear out of Skeiron territory then. They'd have to ride hard, and on this uni-rider, it wouldn't be comfortable.

She fired up the engine with a press of the key fob to a square in the center of the bike. The engine rumbled to life. She double-checked the brakes and rode out, pulling away from the gambling hall into the dead of night. The moons were giving less illumination than nights past.

Please don't let a storm come up.

"Tuck that tube back in my pouch on the belt, Jack."

He followed her directions, though where she might experience arousal from his hands on her, all she felt was worry.

"I'm sorry, but we have maybe an hour or two before they marshal all the forces they want to throw at chasing us down. This rider has a full battery, but to get out of the territory—"

"Just do it. Don't worry about me." He barked the words at her. No doubt the pain was horrendous.

"Fine, but if I go faster…"

"I said it's okay. Hell, I still don't understand why you didn't leave me after I got caught."

Shannon realized in that moment the thought hadn't crossed her mind. Not for one second had she given priority to her own survival, even if she tried to pretend otherwise. No, she'd seen Jack as necessary to her existence. The goal was they both got out alive, not one without the other.

But I can't admit that. "Like I said before, no way Drag would give me full payment if I didn't come back with you. It's not a big deal. Business decision."

He wrapped his arms around her mid-section and squeezed a little tighter. "Sure. What about the hauler?"

"We can't go back for it. It's not on our way back and I think our best bet is to move forward. Back toward Wespero."

Jack was silent for a minute, no doubt playing out possibilities. Finally, he replied, "You're driving and I'm officially lame so it's your call."

"Then hold on tight." She increased her speed, racing across the dirt. They had more freedom of movement than in the hauler. The bonus agility helped because Skeiron territory seemed to have more boulders randomly tossed around the terrain, along with an assortment of prickly bushes and skittering wildlife.

She silently prayed they wouldn't run into any slithers either. Though she swore she'd seen one or two slinking across the ground. Hard to tell if her eyes were playing tricks or not.

They weren't generating much heat but moving fast would hopefully reduce the risk. She started running through scenarios, but the only one that made sense was to get back to the Trading Post at Argest. Old Beard would have access to a synthesizer.

They needed the tech because Jack wasn't going to make it all the way back to Frog Lick in his current condition. The leg had given out, then he'd wrenched it. He was running a fever. If she'd left him…

He'd be dead.

Her chest hurt at the idea. There wasn't a future she wanted where Jack wasn't alive. Frog Lick needed him. She needed him. *Shit.* Except she had other needs. The flash…the Macintosh hired mercenary wasn't going to just stop coming for her. She didn't want to bring that trouble to Jack's door.

She'd fix her problems, then come back, right?

Jack groaned anew. She needed to quit worrying about anything past tonight—getting to the Trading

Post and keeping Jack alive—that was all that mattered…for now.

Chapter Sixteen

Argest Trading Post was still lit up when she pulled the uni-rider to a halt in front of it. Here they were again, at the mercy of Old Beard, and she had nothing to trade this time.

"Shannon," Jack mumbled. He had started leaning hard against her the last hour, fading in and out of consciousness. She'd done her best to stay upright and keep the rider moving along with keeping him on the bike.

"What's up? I'm going to go inside and negotiate a place for us."

Jack patted his leg. "My pocket, flash."

She hopped off the bike, careful to leave him in place, gently easing him down until he draped over the entire thing. Then she dug into his pocket. The flash she pulled out was wrinkled and crumpled together.

She stifled a laugh. "You took the betting from the table?"

"It was on the floor, already wadded up. Someone else had tried to make off with it. Figured it might help." His words were sleepy, his eyes closed.

"And you don't break the rules." She pressed a kiss against his forehead.

"Never said I don't...but I prefer not to. Hated that place."

Skeiron was definitely a gang-town she'd prefer to never visit again, but she was still mesmerized by this man. But there was no time to fawn over him when he needed her help—the fever was getting worse. She charged off and into the Trading Post.

Old Beard was wiping down the bar. "Last call was twenty minutes ago. Kicking everyone out."

She slipped two pieces of crinkle onto the bar top, the gold shining brightly. "I need the room for another night. And someone to help me carry my companion to it."

"Interesting." Old Beard stroked the long, wiry bush of hair on his chin. "Afraid I don't have the room. Someone else already paid for it. Got a hut, around the back. A couple cots in there, some blankets. Nothing fancy."

"And the help?"

Old Beard called over a younger man. "Help this woman get her things into the hut."

Shannon slid more crinkle across the wood bar. "I need water, food and a synthesizer too."

"Let's ask for a Mars moon as well? You come in here demanding a lot for so late at night."

She was tired of playing, exhaustion had started to work on her as well. There wasn't time for games. "And I'm willing to pay for it, unlike last time. You got the flash. If you don't have the product, then just say."

Old Beard swiped the crinkle away before she could grab it back. "You have young Cross help you settle into the hut. Send him back here after and I'll have him bring you what you requested."

She nodded in agreement, then headed for the door. Right at the entrance she paused. "Throw in some painkiller too."

Old Beard scoffed and waved her away.

Outside, Jack was half hanging on the rider.

"Shit." She ran to him, Cross following her, and got Jack steady again. He was completely out. "Cross, keep him steady as I guide the rider around to the hut."

They were silent, for the most part, but slow moving under Jack's weight. When they finally got to the ramshackle building, Shannon set about preparing the room. She fired up the small heating element inside, put her torch and belt on the small table and wiped at the one of the cots with her bare hands, trying to bat away as much red dust as she could from its surface.

The next bit was the most difficult. It took both her and Cross to carry Jack, half-dragging him to the cot. They got him there after plenty of groans and readjustments.

"He don't look okay, lady." These were the most words this young man had said to her so far.

"He's not. Run back to the Trading Post and bring the other things I bought from Old Beard."

As soon as Cross left, she set to work, covering Jack up. She checked the canister of nanites and tried her best not to glance too longingly at the other cot.

"I'm just so damn tired."

"Lady?"

Shannon glanced over her shoulder to see Cross in the open doorway, hands and arms full of items. She stood up. "Just ignore me. It's been a long day. Let me help."

She arranged everything on the table, then fired up the synthesizer to ensure it worked.

"Beard included this, too. Said you might want it if you planned on an injection." Cross held up a wrapped syringe and needle packet.

She snatched it out of his hands and inspected it closely. "Good, large-enough gauge. That's all we need, Cross...except, can you plug up the uni-rider to charge?"

He gave a nod. "Sure thing. Be ready before sunup tomorrow."

Then he was gone. Shannon shut and bolted the door. No more people, no more interruptions.

There were grunts and moans behind her. She pivoted to see Jack starting to thrash from side to side. He'd throw himself off the cot if he got too rowdy.

"No." She quickly moved to his side and held his arms down until he quieted. He was covered in sweat, the fever still present, skin hot to the touch. They needed the nanites.

Over the next hour, she worked on the synthesizer, pouring the nanites into two separate tubes, drawing blood from Jack's arm and mixing the two to ensure they were compatible. No explosions, no degradation. She took the mixture and injected it into Jack.

At that point, the hard work was done. She sat on the ground next to his cot doing her best to keep her eyes open, and eventually was unable to stay awake. She'd trade anything to ensure this worked, that he lived. The way he smiled at her, believed in her...how he'd gone against his own instincts and done things he disliked to keep them safe.

The way he said her name, how he'd looked when he was coming. Those memories played through her mind in a loop until she passed out.

She awoke to sunlight filtering in through cracks in the wood and an endless banging on the door.

"One minute," she choked out. Her voice was hoarse, throat bone dry. She jumped to her feet, remembering where she was.

Jack...was breathing steady. No more fever and sleep heaving. *Thank the worlds.*

The banging continued. She grabbed a canister of water, wrenched the top off and downed half of it.

I'll buy more.

They still had flash, plenty to spend for whatever they needed. She made her way to the door, flung the bolt and cracked it open. Cross stood on the other side.

"Any reason for all that banging?"

"Sorry." He pointed to the Trading Post. "Old Beard says he needs to see you right away. Something important."

"No other details?"

Cross shook his head. But Shannon didn't miss the way he rocked back and forth between his feet. Nervous and fidgety.

"Tell him I'll be right there."

Had to be the Skeirons had chased them past their borders. One thing the gang-towns of Auster would unite under was disliking those from other territories. Old Beard had sold her out, or the presence of the uni-rider did.

Either way...she needed a weapon and didn't have one. At least not one with bullets. She pulled the two-shooter from her belt and decided to go with that. Jack still slept peacefully. At the very least, she'd leave the flash with him and when he came to, he'd be able to get out. Go back to Frog Lick.

If they don't demand his blood, too.

She carefully closed the door to the hut and made her way around to the front entrance to the Trading Post, expecting to find an army waiting for her. Instead, there were nothing but a couple haulers.

Strange.

Her fears lessened a small bit. Maybe she was seeing enemies where there were none. She needed to quit jumping to the worst possible scenario, even when her mind felt the need. Trotting up the small flight of stairs, she swung open the double doors and walked through, calling out to Old Beard.

"You woke me from my slumber for what, old man..." The words died on her lips, because there stood the second biggest threat she needed to be worried about. The mercenary in all black.

They didn't have the cover of darkness on their side this time, but they were still gender neutral in dress and appearance. Shannon couldn't make heads or tails of this, because seeing her opponents' eyes, face and looks made it easier to read them. This person wasn't built that way, only revealing their eyes, which glowed even in daylight, a shimmering yellow.

Covered in fabric head to toe, the mercenary beckoned to Shannon. "Here, as we determined. You're past due."

"We?" Then Shannon saw the other two. Bulky men, in thin shirts and threadbare jackets. Bridget's twin bruisers that she liked to deploy for extra intimidation whenever she could. "Oh, yeah...it's taking a bit longer."

"Then what do we take in return?"

The twins grinned and glanced at each other. They were identical except their scars. One had a permanent burn mark on his forehead that trailed down his cheek. The other had a faded scar around his mouth where someone had tried to make his grin wider. They'd shared plenty of stories while she'd played cards.

Then they'd given her a few punches for being caught with a couple extra pocketed hearts. She didn't care to be on the receiving end of those punches again.

"I got nothing to give."

The mercenary moved fast, lightning fucking fast, snatching her up then pinning her against the nearest table. "Body parts work."

No one would fucking save her now. This beastly person didn't care about humanity or help. Just about delivering for the person who paid their salary.

"Check my pockets," Shannon grunted.

The mercenary positioned Shannon's legs wide, and used sharp, thick needles to spear her clothes to the wood. Shannon was spread-eagled in less than thirty seconds and unable to move. Only then was she thoroughly searched. Her clothes remained on, but she still felt violated at the rough handling of her person.

She wanted to scream, cry out, but those types of pleas tended to embolden her attacker and wouldn't gain her any sympathy. Swallowing hard, she fought back against the tightness in her throat, the tears that wanted to come. *My way…I go my way.*

The members of Argest present kept a wide berth. She saw a few, including Cross. No clue about Old Beard since the bar was behind her.

The shooter landed on the table with a clack and a thud.

"An empty weapon doesn't cover the debt."

Shannon grunted. "Yeah, I know. But two days? Does this give me two days to finish getting what she wanted?"

"Maybe a few hours, but these." The mercenary leaned over her, deliberately putting their weight on her, showing how powerless she was here.

A thin, sharp knife appeared in the mercenary's hand and Shannon's breaths grew shorter as the blade moved under her left pinky nail, then into the bed.

Shannon screamed, unable to be silent against the pain, then the nail popped off. Her flesh burned, nerve endings lighting up. The mercenary kept going until all the fingernails on her left hand were gone. Something had coated the blade separating the nail from flesh and cauterized her exposed beds. But the agony had tears streaming down her face.

She struggled against each one in futility and started to fight more, her mumbled "no's" and panicked "stops" growing more high pitched as the mercenary moved to her right hand. The lack of control to stop this from happening, her inability to fight against this force, made her angry.

So fucking angry and desperate. The people around her were cowards, but the lesson wasn't lost. No one helped people like her. No one cared.

When the mercenary was done, they removed the pins holding Shannon in place, then collected the nails in a bag and handed them to the burned twin. "These will give you three days. After that, you don't have what you promised, and we take your head."

Shannon collapsed to the floor and pushed herself up to lean against a table leg. Her cheeks were hot, throat tight from her cries. Chest heaving, humiliation like a cold, invisible shroud over her.

She longed to disappear or run, anything to escape the moment, but there was no escape. Instead, she forced herself to look at her violator and any others in the room, willing her body to stop shuddering, to stay strong. To refuse anyone the satisfaction of seeing how much all of this hurt.

"Three days... My nails are worth more than half a week."

"You're not in a place to negotiate." The mercenary motioned the twins toward the door before they started to follow. "For your sake, you better deliver."

"Oh, I'll deliver." *You straight to hell.*

Once they made their exit, all her summoned strength left her. She slumped against the table, head hung in shame. The last time she'd been this disgraced had been at the hands of her father, who had given her a public beating for daring to ask why she wasn't allowed to play with other children. Then it was the same as now. No one dared to help her. Either because they believed she deserved what she received or because they didn't have the strength to stand up against poor behavior.

Minutes passed and she did her best to wipe the tears away on her covered forearms. She struggled to get off the floor and put herself in a chair. Her fingers were hot, like they were on fire. A small cup with a couple of pills, and a bottle of clear liquid was sat in front of her, along with a bag of rags.

"I didn't—"

"You look like you need it." Old Beard took a seat across from her. "Let me bandage these up for you."

She frowned, kicking back the pills and washing them down with the sharp sting of vodka. Not the cheap stuff either. "I'm not paying you more flash."

"And I wouldn't ask you to. Lay your hands out flat. I'll clean them and get you fixed up."

She chuckled sarcastically. "Oh, yeah and what debt will I owe?"

"Nothing."

No... "That's not how this world works and I fucking know it."

"For once, Zephyr, stop fighting. I'm not going to add to the hurt."

Those were the last words she remembered besides the urge to stab the fucker in the face and anyone else who kept lying to her. *When I wake.*

* * * *

Voices murmuring. Banging nearby. The thud of something hard hitting dirt. Jack was about ready to call out that people were being too damn loud in the mechanics bay on his nap time.

Then he took a good, deep breath. The scent in the air was not as iron rich. Dirt, musty scents of something that had been wet and mildewed, old wood.

Not the bay.

His eyes shot open, and that was when the memories came back. The game with the Skeirons. He'd gotten into a fight. Twisted his damn leg...and so much fucking pain. Shannon had been there and saved him, getting them out of there on a uni-rider that had been annoying but the buzz of the combustion engine and the constant vibration of his ass had dulled the agony for a bit.

They'd made it to the Trading Post then he'd passed out...again.

A habit I need to start breaking.

But the pain wasn't as strong. No, he only had a twinge. He cast off the old, hole-riddled blanket covering him and lifted his leg. He bent the knee a couple times, spread wide. There were still some aches, but nothing like before when he thought the damn thing was a fire going to eat him alive and the weight of the cybernetic component had become so heavy he could barely lift it.

The voices were louder, closer.

Where is Shannon?

Jack stood up and crept over to the door of this small building he was in. Listening for any reference to what these men creeping around outside were looking for. Shannon had said something about the Skeirons coming after them. Had they decided to chase beyond their territory?

"Hexa was told not to take excuses this time."

Fuck, he hated this damn shack. The wood slats were actually assembled as if someone cared about their job, barely a crack available for Jack to peek out of.

The other one chuckled. "Yeah, but we have to find the guy. Our informant said she left with someone else from Frog Lick."

He froze. Not Skeiron, but someone else. Someone chasing Shannon. Jack glanced down and saw the bolt. Moving with caution, he slid the bolt shut. Perfect timing, as one of them attempted to open the door.

"Hey, don't make a mess."

The one at the door gave a good shove. The whole shack rattled, but held firm. "He could be hiding in here. Besides, she can pay for damage. That moonie's fault we're in Argest in the first place. Hate this damn place."

They were after Shannon. That confirmed it. But they wanted him too. He needed to find her, needed a weapon. Glancing around he found nothing that would do much damage. Two cots, the crappy blankets, a chair, a table with a synthesizer. There was still some gray sludge in the canister, but it was half gone.

She'd obviously worked to administer what he needed. He grabbed the chair, frantic energy spreading through his limbs along with the feeling he needed to save Shannon. She'd done so much for him already, if she was hurt, or worse…killed.

His chest got tight, like a heavy boulder had taken up space in there. There were few people he'd gotten so emotional about in his life. To have such a feeling again meant Shannon had become important to him. *I'm an idiot.*

He put his hand on the bolt, ready to spring into action, when static echoed through the air, along with a voice. "We're leaving. Abandon the search. Meet back at the haulers."

The men walked off, and Jack waited a couple minutes before he exited the shack. Following along closely, he watched the men, both with close-cropped hair and a distinctive tattoo on the back of their necks. They got into a hauler, while a person covered head to toe in black material and twin hulking men as big as him got into the other hauler. Once they drove off, he made his move.

Charging without a second thought inside the Trading Post, he frantically glanced around for Shannon, who was passed out on a table, her ass in a chair. Old Beard, as she'd called him, sat across from her cleaning her nail beds that were bloodied and burned, with no fingernails.

Guilt racked him, made him stumble a bit as he moved toward them. "What happened?"

"An assassin for hire. Elite, deadly and Miss Zephyr here didn't stand a chance. Pinned her down and took her nails as payment for an extension on whatever she owes, to whomever she owes it." Old Beard didn't even glance at him, his focus all on the cleaning and bandaging for Shannon.

"Is she?"

Old Beard scoffed. "She's tough…too tough to go down because a couple of nails were acid burned off her fingers. I gave her something to knock her out. She already suffered enough losing against that sludge sack Inncukai, figured she didn't deserve to suffer while I bandaged her up."

Jack grabbed a seat and stayed beside her. His mind was a maze of questions about the woman he'd thought he was coming to know.

"Those Inncukai are no joke."

"I've heard stories…" But Jack had only ever seen one. A friend of an old resident of Frog Lick, but that woman didn't look anything like the person he'd watched leave in the hauler.

"Well, she" — Old Beard pointed at Shannon before picking up the last finger to wrap — "got you three days. Suggest you let her get some rest and as soon as she's up, you both take off."

When all of Shannon's fingers had been covered, Jack stood up, to ready to take her back to the shack.

Old Beard gave him a once over. "Looks like you're feeling a lot better than last night. What's the secret?"

"Good metabolism. Had too much to drink last night, let the game go on a little too long." Jack pulled

Shannon's chair back, then crouched to hoist her into his arms.

"Sure, whatever you say. I'll have Cross escort you." He motioned a young man with black hair and dark skin over to them. "Help this fella out to the hut."

"Yes, sir."

Cross held open doors as he was instructed. When they finally got inside the hut and Jack finished laying Shannon down, Cross spoke. "Is she going to be okay? She took a lot of pain, never seen such a thing."

Cross' words cut him deep. Jack had been hiding in a hut while that Inncukai cut on Shannon. He should have helped her, stopped the pain. Because that was what he hadn't been able to do for his mother. Prevent the suffering when all her risk-taking caught up with her.

"Hopefully she'll make a quick recovery. Best way to get there is rest. Thank you, Cross."

The younger man nodded. "Sure thing. Happy to help if you need anything else."

He was gone before Jack could respond, shutting the door behind him. Jack moved to put the bolt in place then turned to face a sleeping Shannon.

Her breaths were steady, slow and restful. Which was good—who knew how much pain she would be in? Pain he couldn't prevent her from having. He felt weak all over again, like he had when he was young and incapable of doing anything but standing by and watching the results of her folly.

He moved to sit by the table hunting through the supplies there for something to eat. They had more bread and those damn food cubes. Little more than mushed protein and supplements designed to meet dietary needs, but with no taste. He missed home,

Gaia's meals at the Watering Hole and the fresh foods from the airponics greenhouses Rune ran.

Soon, he'd make it back. But first he needed to determine what was really happening with Shannon. What had she hidden from all of them? Because Inncukai and those thugs were there for a reason and while there was a slim chance it was for Jack, something told him Shannon had been the true target.

He contemplated more as he ate, washing down the bland taste of the cubes with water and bread, considering all that he knew about Shannon.

When she started to move, he was there right at her side.

"What happened?" she asked, rubbing her eyes then letting out a yelp. "Fuck, my fingers…that sonuvabitch."

"Yeah, afraid you know more than me about what occurred. I'm still wondering why you have an assassin with Macintosh goons chasing after you?" He'd meant to take the conversation slow, to assess how she was feeling, but he couldn't shake the deep unrest and betrayal coursing through him.

"You saw them, then?"

"Kind of hard to miss when they were searching for me as well. Care to tell me why they're after us?"

She kept her eyes on her fingers, moving each one individually to evaluate them. "It's my problem to deal with."

Jack stood and went back to the table, pounding his fist against the wood. Everything rattled, the synthesizer precariously close to the edge. "When they are after someone else, then it's not your problem any longer."

"Don't break that. You still need another shot." She jumped into action, rushing the table and resituating the machine.

"I deserve to know." The words were barely more than a mutter, as Jack crossed his arms to prevent from lashing out at other inanimate objects. This wasn't how things should have been, not after what they'd shared…*after what I confessed.*

She began to mix the rest of the gray goop in a tube, pouring slowly. He didn't miss the way she winced from the pain still generating from her fingers. "Before I came to Frog Lick, I ran into hard times and tried to change my fortune in a few games of chance."

Grabbing a syringe, Shannon held out her hand. "I need to draw a little bit of your blood."

Jack laid his arm out on the table.

"Make a fist, it will be easier that way."

He did as she asked. "You had to have known winning is damn near impossible with Macintosh."

"Eh, winning is difficult anywhere. Sometimes you just need a good run of luck and I didn't have any there." She inserted the needle and the brief pain was welcome, something to think about besides the fact she'd been lying to all of them from the start.

"So, you took the job to get flash."

"To pay off my debt, yeah." She pulled the needle out and pressed a rag to his arm. "Hold that tight."

The blood poured into the tube of gray, then into the synthesizer to blend with a press of a button.

"You never thought you should warn us? Macintosh and Full Throttle are sworn enemies. They'd love a chance to catch one of us away from the flock. Hell, they tried to kill Hemi."

The synthesizer wound down, the spinner slowing. Shannon picked up the tube, gave it a shake, then put it back in for another round. "I'm aware, but what happened to Hemi didn't change my circumstances. And would Drag or Gina have been willing to hire me if I'd confessed I owed money to the very woman who'd hurt one of their own?"

"I don't know." Because truthfully, if a stranger had told any of them they had debt to Macintosh, they would have most likely been given a boot to the backside and shoved out of town.

"You're a horrible liar, Jack." She reached for the tube again, now finished with the second round of mixing. "They would have turned me away."

He wanted to rebut her words but couldn't without lying. The bottom line—"They may have initially, but someone would have argued for you. Probably Gina. You had a skill we needed, and everyone makes mistakes." Even Gina had hidden some secrets of her own when she first came to Frog Lick, though he couldn't share those with Shannon.

"Humbling oneself to people over and over knowing there is a good chance of rejection isn't my style." She inserted the tube into the end of the syringe. "I didn't want to burden anyone else with my problems and I'm afraid I don't know gang politics that much outside of Auster."

Lies. He could tell by the way she didn't look at him, kept to her task instead of making eye contact. There was something else she'd hidden from him and he didn't have the desire to keep debating. He wanted to know, like he'd asked his mother all those years ago to simply tell the truth.

"How bad is it?" *Give her one more chance.*

"Roll up your sleeve?" She motioned to his arm.

He shoved the fabric up, exposing his biceps. Then she plunged the needle in, no ceremony, no warning. He winced.

"Sorry, better to get this over quickly."

"You can tell me the rest of whatever you're holding back. I can handle the truth. In fact, I'd prefer it." The pain from the needle was nothing compared to the ache in his chest. She would break him.

"It's nothing I can't fix. Now, we rest. This last dose of nanites might hit you a bit harder than the first one. The new ones have to fully consume the old."

His skin was already starting to get hot. "Fine. But we talk when we get up."

"Whatever, strip."

"What?" he asked as he stood, holding onto the table for stability.

Shannon touched the edge of his shirt and started to lift. "Take them off. We need to reduce your heat, not add to it."

He took over and she stepped away, moving across the small space to push two cots together, then grabbed a couple of the cleaner blankets. Then she took off her clothes as well.

"Are you hot too?" he asked as he lay down on the cot.

She climbed onto the other cot and pulled a blanket over her. "I want to be free for a spell. Forget how powerless that clothing made me." She'd suffered in the last few hours, in ways that would stick to a person. Make them feel weak.

He couldn't help, except… He held his hand out for hers. She placed one finger-tip-bandaged hand, the fingers themselves still red and irritated. "You don't have to suffer alone."

"Alone is what I'm good at."

Though she said the words, she kept her hand in his as they both drifted off to sleep.

Chapter Seventeen

Shannon woke to the call of a coyote in the middle of the night. She stilled herself and blinked repeatedly, trying to make sense of what was happening. That was when she realized Jack had rotated to his side and scooted to the edge of his cot sometime during sleep. He had a hand on her bare breast, and her hand no longer linked with his. Instead her palm rested against his rock-hard cock.

No fever, but warmth. She couldn't help but stroke him, even if her fingers ached a bit with the motion. She turned her head and her gaze clashed with Jack's. His eyes wide open, he licked his lips. The heat there told her he was thinking the same thing.

There still a lot unsaid, words she couldn't vocalize and secrets she didn't want to confess. Because she didn't want to see this look in his eyes, the passion there disappear. Or the caring, concerned Jack melt away.

But all things would eventually come to an end. Until then, she'd take whatever he wanted to give.

He massaged her breast, kneading the flesh, then pinching her nipple. She moaned, arching into his touch as she tried to match the pressure with her hand wrapped around his cock.

"Come here," he whispered.

She let go of her hold and let him wrap his arms around her, pulling her over to his cot. He kicked the blanket off of him and settled her atop his body. Their lips met, kisses that turned into entanglement of tongues.

Rushed and frantic. As if they were chasing after something fleeting. She wanted all of him, hard and fast.

"Ride me," he said against her ear, nipping at the lobe.

She sat up then, rocking her body upward by pushing her palms against his chest. He assisted her, holding her up by her hips. There was enough room for her to grip and guide him into her snug heat. She was so wet, but she rubbed his cock against her entrance, teasing them both.

He flung his head backward, only to pump upward into her palm.

"Yes," she hissed, as she plunged down at the same time.

In less than a second, he was seated inside her. She loved the fullness, how he completely overwhelmed her. She was so caught up in the moment of connection she just sat there. He was the one who got them moving again, lifting her up and down as if she weighed nothing.

She joined in then, chasing the breath out of her very body as she met each surge of his hips with a drop of her own.

Before long, she found release, but he wasn't done. No, he flipped her onto her back and started to move anew. He speared his hands into her hair, gently tugging against her curls. Then with each penetration he spoke, the words low and rough.

"I made the necklace you wore."

She gasped.

"I always believed the idea my soulmate would find it." Jack picked up his pace

His confession paired with his movements were reaching into her from two different places, captivating her mind and her body.

"But that can't be you."

Tears gathered in the corners of her eyes. The strokes kept the pleasure mounting, even as he flayed her with his words.

"Can't be because the universe wouldn't allow me to sacrifice my heart to a woman who is the representation of everything I despise...lies, risk, carelessness."

He kept moving, staring deep into her eyes, the anguish there blurred by the tears she couldn't stop. He kissed her lips, then lapped those tears with his tongue, as if licking the evidence of her physical pain away might change things.

Only then did she notice he was crying too. How could an act that felt so wonderful, the joining between them, be marred with such anguish? The climb to her release wasn't abating. He moved faster then. Every nerve ending in her body was alive and seeking relief.

Her chest hurt, her throat was tight and still her orgasm burst forth, along with Jack's. They were both left panting, sweaty messes, clutching each other as if they were a lifeline. She hated how her natural state was something he despised.

She put a death sentence on any idea of voicing the truth, because if she told him why she'd come to Frog Lick in the first place... *It doesn't matter anymore.*

Jack pressed his lips to her forehead, her cheeks, her nose, then kissed her long and deep. She choked against that meeting of lips at first, trying her best not to start crying again. But she embraced the joining because she wanted this moment even as she worried it might be the last.

Then he pulled back, whispering what she never expected. "Through all that, I love you. Shannon, I care for you with a deep need I don't want and can't stop."

She opened her mouth but words froze on her tongue. No amount of swallowing and trying again could get anything to come out. Who had ever confessed love for her? Caring, sure. A fondness, yes. But outright love...when he swore she wasn't the one for him in nearly the same breath?

What did it mean to be wanted and hated at the same time? Did she fight for or against him?

He pulled his softening cock from her body, then shifted so he was once again on his back. "I won't hold you here, if you need space."

She spread her arms around his torso, embracing him closely, as she pressed her cheek to his chest. "I think it will be best to sleep right here."

She had a desire to feel his heartbeat, the slow inhale and exhale as he breathed. To know the man beneath her loved her... She still wasn't sure how to process those feelings or respond to them. Though she was thankful for his presence, his caring...even if he'd made her cry. *The jerk.*

This connection between them calmed her in a way she'd come to miss when they parted.

Unless I tell him everything.

Even then, he'd hate her. There was no way forward for them, even if he loved her. She fell asleep trying to envision a future where he still loved her after he discovered why she'd really shown up in his life.

* * * *

Shannon woke back on her own cot. Rolling over, the pain still present in her fingertips, she found Jack fully clothed and testing out his leg.

Crouching low, jumping up, bending, stretching.

"It's holding up?" she asked, reaching for her clothing on the floor, trying to dismiss how those clothes had betrayed her against the Inncukai. She was still bothered by the events of yesterday compounded by Jack's confession the previous night and she wasn't quite sure where things stood.

Fear kept her from asking. Somewhere along this journey into her past life, she'd gotten used to companionship and the idea of having someone around to have her back. In Humans First, she'd believed in the lies of the bond between group members when in reality their faux support paled in comparison to what Jack had given her thus far.

Sex, conversation, care and even the offer of protection, if not the act of it. *I can't blame him for not being there yesterday morning.*

"Yeah, there's no pain and I can do everything I did before. If not more. No way to know the extent of my capabilities until I'm back in Frog Lick."

"Right." She pulled her shirt over her head and put her arms in. "If we leave soon, we could reach the territory border by nightfall."

Jack sighed, hanging his head. When he finally looked at her, there was something different in his gaze, closed off and nothing like the level of emotion he'd delivered last night.

"Don't look at me like that, please. I know I didn't say anything in response to your declaration, but—"

"I never expected you to." He sighed again, as if marshaling himself toward something. "This is where we part ways, Shannon. Gina can synthesize the nanites herself, using the same technique you used on me for the others."

Shannon shut her mouth and opened it again, trying to summon words that made sense.

He's leaving me. I'm not enough or too much... Love is a lie.

"What about my payment?" She refused to let him see her as weak, even if her heart was hardening all over again. He'd brought her to a low place where she'd been emotionally exposed and he wanted to dismiss whatever they'd exchanged the night before. "I was getting paid good money to finish this job and save you and your buddies."

"Didn't you want the plans to the racer instead?"

She froze mid-zipping her pants, turning her back to Jack. Well and truly caught, with a good dose of shame lashing her body like a cold wind.

"I won't lie, that's what Macintosh asked of me, in exchange to clear my debt. You're not wrong that

Bridget has a hard-on for sticking it to Full Throttle." She turned to face him. "Except, the further along we got into this, the more I searched for another way."

He sighed. "I want to believe, but I can't. You'd say anything to get the results you want. You say what you need people to hear so they'll go along with plans. I've watched you over this last week. You've trained yourself too well."

Shannon's arms hung limp at her sides. She tried to ignore the hard lump taking up residence in the dead center of her chest, like a rock weighing her down. She'd been this way for so long, doing her best to survive in a world that didn't give a shit about her. Watching people get spat out for things they had no control over. She didn't know how to be anything else.

When she didn't speak, Jack continued. "As far as I'm concerned, it's best we split ways here. I'm not risking bringing those Macintosh thugs chasing you to Frog Lick. If you want money, you can get it from Drag at the next Wespero regional race in a few weeks."

"If I live that long," she mumbled. She would never admit how much fear ran through her veins at the idea of moving forward alone. The damn Inncukai assassin had her pinned to a table in under a minute. *Imagine it will take less time to kill me.*

He gathered the tube that still held a tiny bit of the nanites in his hands and pocketed it. "Do I risk everyone I love for one person?"

"But you said you loved me too." And he'd told her he despised her as well. What emotion won out in a situation like that? She knew what her answer would have been. *Hate...because ultimately I hated my father more than I ever loved him.*

Except she didn't despise Jack. This was the first true action he'd taken against her, and it would whittle her chances of survival down to practically nothing.

She frowned, clenching her fists and pounding them against her thighs. "This is so easy for you, isn't it? That whole bit about soulmates and fate, this fucking necklace."

Shannon reached under her collar and pulled the piece of bone into the light, the etched lines darker, and she ripped the damn thing off her neck. The sting as the hemp rope dragged against her skin was welcome. She'd free herself of this mess. When she tossed the necklace at him, Jack didn't catch it, just let it drop to the floor.

"I'm taking the uni-rider and heading to Frog Lick today."

"You're not listening to me. How dare you play with my feelings? You lied. People who say they love someone don't leave them. They stay. They fight. If you cared about me, wouldn't you try and save me?"

Jack chuckled darkly, the mask on his face so similar to the looks of disdain he'd cast her way when they first met. "You're one to talk... People who love people, who care about them, they open up about their problems. They don't lie and hide truths until it's too late and you can't drag them back from the hell they've created for themselves. I can't save you, Shannon. Only you can do that. All the love I have for you, the very ache in my bone marrow that wants to wrap you in my arms and never let you go, can't possibly stop the storm you've brought to your door. I've been in this fight before, trying to save another woman who wore that necklace." He pointed to the bone on the dirt floor. "I'm starting to think the damn thing is cursed… You can keep it."

He walked to the door then, pulled back the bolt and threw the piece of wood wide. Each sound was like a death knell, signaling the end of something she'd never get back.

"You're wrong, you know!" she yelled after his retreating frame, even as she dove to scoop up the necklace.

She marched after him, tying it back around her neck. No way would he win, would he jinx her. "It's not a curse. It's a blessing, a good omen, and I'll make you regret walking away from me. You'll wish you'd taken me with you."

She stopped about four steps away from the door of the hut, but he kept moving, not once looking back at her or bothering to respond to her words. His ability to stand by his convictions was both inspiring and heartbreaking. Those words he'd deployed, how he couldn't save her, only she could save herself…

Damn him.

Because he was right. She'd lost herself a bit and needed to remember she'd survived plenty without help. With the grip of her hands and the gray matter in her head, she would solve her own damn problems instead of heaping them on Jack's muscular back. When she was done, she'd make him beg for her.

Maybe it's better… This way he won't get himself killed like he almost did with those Skeirons. She'd gotten out of that mess. She'd find a way to solve her Macintosh problem.

Planting her hands on her hips, she watched in righteous fury as he drove off. She'd show him.

Chapter Eighteen

Every part of his body wanted to pivot the wheels of the uni-rider, turn around and go back to her. To do as he'd said.

All the love I have for you, the very ache in my bone marrow that wants to wrap you in my arms and never let you go...

But the feelings he possessed for her...the deep-seated need to see her smile, to watch her challenge idiots to games of chance or even to let her chase pleasure atop of him however she demanded didn't negate the biggest problem between them.

...can't possibly stop the storm you've brought to your door.

This was the ultimatum he'd set for himself, and he couldn't back down now. She had to fight her own battle. Only then would he know for sure that she wouldn't destroy his heart over and over again. He'd challenged her to prove she could change. To break the cycle of her errors, maybe wake up and realize she didn't need to take such risks to survive. There were other ways to joy-ride existence than putting her life on the line every single time.

His mother had taunted fate the same way Shannon did and he couldn't stick around for that. He recollected his father, how his mother's gambling losses had repeatedly torn him down until the man he'd admired became a hollowed-out shell, the fight ripped out of him to the point it had almost killed him and Jack.

Jack shook his head, willing the memories of that fateful day in the mines away. He had some regrets from that day, including not knocking his dad out and carrying the stubborn man away before the collapse. Maybe his father would still be alive, and just maybe…his mother would have stayed.

Those types of thoughts kept making him question the decision to leave Shannon. Should he have stayed and tried harder, stood by her side? He fought those ideas even as he passed the territory border with the sun setting.

He pushed through, making only a couple of stops along the way. Without the pain in his leg, it wasn't hard to find the fortitude to keep going. Maybe another side-effect of the nanites?

Jack would ask Gina to run some tests when he got back. This second-generation work might have some added benefits.

The moons were high by the time he reached Frog Lick. He was starving, thirsty and so happy to see the pillars of steam from the hydroponics warehouse, the lights in the windows, the rows of houses, the mechanics bay. This was home and he'd never been happier to see these familiar buildings.

There might have been times he'd dreamed of traveling to different territories and even off-world, but after actually leaving, he'd found himself homesick for everyday habits and places. Even now, his mouth craved Gaia's stew made with the vegetables grown in Rune's airponics gardens and ale brewed from the hops and barley. No place could beat the comforts they'd established here in Frog Lick.

Exactly why we need to win the race.

He rode into town not at all disappointed at how quiet the streets were. It was past last call. Still, the mechanics bay main door flew open right as he brought the uni-rider to a stop.

"I've done all I can. Now we wait for someone to test it. If he's not back in a couple days, then I'll climb in the damn thing myself." Drag's voice echoed over to Jack as their leader walked out of the mechanics bay then came to a dead stop when he saw him. "Jack."

"Jack?" Snapper said, jogging out of the building.

Others followed — Gina, Rune and Hemi. His family all piled out of the building and surrounded him. Questions fired off a mile a minute.

"How did it go?"

"Did you get the nanites?"

"Are you hungry?"

"Thirsty?"

"You bastard, we were worried… Where's Shannon?"

Of course Hemi asked the last question, which Jack chose to ignore.

"The trip was a success. I have the solution to our problems, and I'm starving. Think Gaia will feed me?"

A chorus of agreement and celebration rose up around him and the group near forced him toward the

Watering Hole. They were eager for information but appeared more worried about his health and the fact he was alive.

Instead of continuing to ask him things, the group gathered around as he sat and ate. They told him what had happened in the week he'd been gone for the rework on the engine. A couple tweaks, according to Gina.

"You know her, can't stop finetuning," Snapper said as he hugged her close to him.

She sat on his lap and pressed a kiss to his cheek. "Shush, you like the way I can find efficiencies. Besides, it's logical to always seek improvement."

An image of Shannon popped in his memory, her pressing a kiss to him, her grin. So similar to Gina's and yet different.

But I left her.

"Yes, everything is ready for you to give it a run through," Drag replied, passing a brand-new mug of ale across the table. "And we have the bonus of Hemi getting a wife."

"What the he-he-he—" Jack coughed on his last swallow of stew and started hacking to clear the broth he'd tried to inhale.

"Yeah, within three nights of you gone," Snapper chimed in. "Idiot got himself hitched by Proxy."

"The guitarist?" Jack wheezed that question then grabbed the glass of water in front of him and chugged it.

Gina chuckled. "Yes, Proxy is a wedding magistrate. He conducted it right there on the stage. Rune and I acted as witnesses."

Hemi cleared his throat, and everyone looked in his direction. "Enough about that. I'd appreciate if you left

Sophia out of this conversation. There are more important things we should discuss. The nanites? Why Shannon isn't here?"

"I already got the nanites inside me. All we have to do now is have Gina draw some of my blood to mix up injections for the rest of you." Jack chose to completely ignore the second question because he wasn't ready to discuss Shannon. A slight wave of nausea hit him, and he ignored it by shoveling more stew in his mouth.

"He should have tests first, though." This came from Rune, Drag's younger brother.

"I completely agree." Gina slapped her palm on the table and a bit of stew splashed out of Jack's bowl and hit his hand.

Does she have food tonight?

Damn, he needed to stop thinking of her.

"A double check of vitals wouldn't be a bad thing." Jack tried to act like he was as invested in this conversation as everyone else, but it was easier to keep shoveling food or drink into his mouth. Though doing so had an opposite effect because then his mind wandered to Shannon. His stomach ached a bit, though the food was fine, all because he was trying to eat away his own frustration.

"You still haven't said what happened to Shannon," Hemi said, just loud enough Jack could hear him. His face was all worry lines and a grimace as if someone had died. Jack would have to say something, at some point.

"Does it matter?" Snapper leaned in and gave Jack a gentle shove. "This guy got the nanites. We don't need her. With these, we'll get you back in action, Hemi. Even your new wife will be happy about that. Gina can work up a new physical therapy plan. And we save a little money."

Jack tapped his spoon against the bowl to get everyone's attention. "Not exactly. I told Shannon when we parted ways that she could find Drag at the next race to collect the rest of what she's owed."

A look of relief spread across Hemi's entire frame. His shoulders relaxed and he took a nice long drink. "So, she's alive."

"Of course she's alive. But maybe you shouldn't be so concerned about another woman who's not your wife?" Snapper was answering for Jack. He'd never seen the mechanic so buoyant, as if he refused to let anything kill this semi-celebration.

"Love of a good woman and the support of a family will do that for a man." Those were words his father had said before. Where they came from now, Jack didn't know. He'd fucked up, though.

"Yeah, I'll keep to my own business then. Besides, our Jack is one of the good ones. He made the right choice, I'm sure." Those were Hemi's last words on the topic. The fellow driver got up and walked off.

Drag frowned at his departure, but Jack got it. Hemi had warned Jack before he'd left, had practically begged him not to chase Shannon away.

"He liked her a lot," Drag said.

Gina nodded. "She was the only one who didn't treat him differently since the accident… Well, until Sophia showed up."

"Hey." Snapper was back to his jovial touches. "We can't let Hemi ruin the mood. Jack's back, our brother. We need to celebrate, be happy."

The conversation rotated then to their successful, shared memories. Jack finished his bowl of stew, another mug of ale, then Gaia kicked them out. They all piled out of the Watering Hole so Gaia could officially clean up and actually get a good night's rest.

Snapper and Gina made their way back to the mechanics bay. Rune went home to his Petal. Drag lingered a moment.

"Are you good? You seemed a little distant in there."

Jack thought about telling the truth but couldn't. Not to Drag. "Really, I'm exhausted and...I never thought I'd miss this place as much as I did."

Drag smiled at him, a lightening to his eyes even in the low light. "I'm glad you missed us. Glad this place has become a home for you as much as the rest of us."

Jack clapped Drag on his shoulder and tried to ignore the sting on his palm from hitting cybernetic metal. "You're doing a good job. Now I'll work on making sure we finish it, get that championship."

Drag nodded, but didn't respond, just walked off into the night, down the street and into his quarters. Jack headed to his place as well. His small two-bedroom shack was something that had been handed to him by his family. He'd lived there since he'd been born and had hoped to bring home...

"Fuck," he swore under his breath. He locked his hand around the doorknob but he didn't want to turn it.

"Suggest you open the door so we can have this conversation inside versus out." Hemi's deep bass was like a low growl from an invisible predator.

Jack opened the door. "You've got questions, I'll answer them."

He left it ajar so Hemi could follow him inside. Jack lit a lamp and turned the heat element on low. Since the injections, he'd found himself not as cold as he used to feel. The tests that Gina had suggested were definitely needed.

He heard the lock click, then Hemi said, "Tell me what you did and why she didn't come back."

* * * *

Shannon tipped back another shot and closed one eye to get the card numbers to stop doubling. She'd decided after Jack ran off the best way to get a ride was to earn some money. The Trading Post offered several options for her to get crinkle, though the easiest choice had been a poker game.

Wasn't long before she was up, big. Though of course she didn't turn down a drink or five. No, the booze numbed the ache in her chest at Jack being gone. Let her push away the memories. Those words he'd said, all of them had cut like a thousand knives into her flesh. Hurt worse than the nails she'd lost. Though the booze helped numb the pain she still had there too.

Quit lying, me.

"Is the bet to me?" Shannon closed her left eye, then switched for the right eye. She had at least three of kind. Enough to get the job done since this group of three, including the bartender, Old Beard, had seemed to be shit with cards. She almost felt bad for beating them so soundly, but the flash was needed if she wanted to get out of here.

"Yeah, woman. Hurry up." This was from the bad-teeth nothing that had given her the darts her first stay in Argest.

She shoved all her crinkle into the center. "All in."

A couple of the men growled, including Bad-Teeth, and they bowed out. All that was left was Old Beard, who stroked that beard and eyed her speculatively. "You're certain."

Shannon nodded as she tried to pour another shot of whatever they kept giving her into her mouth. A little bit of the liquid dribbled down her chin. "Yep."

Old Beard shoved his stake in and laid his cards down. "Straight flush."

Shannon slapped her own cards down. "Three of kind, bitches."

She started to grab the pot when Old Beard wrenched her hand away, and she hissed at the contact to wounds on the tips of her fingers. "Hey, that's mine."

"Girlie, you lost. You're so drunk you don't even realize."

"I'll play another, win it back." She yanked her hand away from him, not caring how much it fucking hurt. A glance showed blood seeping through the bandage on her middle finger. She held up the bloody finger, flipping Old Beard off. "You re-opened the wound. Least you can do is give me a chance to win the crinkle to replace these bandages."

Old Beard shook his head in dismay. "You don't know when to quit. The luck's gone for you, girl. This kind of crap is exactly why you have that Inncukai after you. Just take the loss. I'll let you sleep in the hut, get a clear head and try again tomorrow."

"I don't have after tomorrow," she replied with a self-deprecating chuckle.

"You're drunk."

"One round." She poured another shot and downed it as Old Beard contemplated her. Sleep would have been nice, but she needed crinkle. The means to survive were up to her. She wouldn't lose now.

Reaching for her talisman of luck, her necklace, she touched it. Straightaway the words came back, his words.

Damn thing is cursed, you can keep it.

Has he ruined it for me?

She shook her head refusing to let Jack win or ruin what she'd done for years. "I go out on my terms," she mumbled.

"Fine. One card," Old Beard said, as he grabbed all the cards and started to shuffle them. The sound made her stomach curdle. The last shot had probably been one too many.

He set the deck in front of him after the fourth shuffle. "Here's how this works. You tell me if the card is red or black. If you guess right, you win the entire pot. You guess wrong, you're doing dishes and scrubbing floors until the job is done."

"It's black." Like her life, constantly dark with no light. She was poison to goodness, evidenced by how she'd killed her mother. How she'd scared Jack away.

Old Beard pulled the card and held it up for everyone to see before he showed it to her. A bright red four told her all she needed to know. She let her head drop to the table and started to laugh at the absurdity of everything. How she was here, playing games, taking risks as Jack said she did. Like his mother, he'd said.

He'd cursed the necklace and now it was coming true. Doomed to be cleaning for Old Beard. She kept laughing and when she lifted her head, Old Beard was giving directions to the young man, Cross. Only this time she noticed the scars on his face, the way he swayed on his feet while standing still. She gagged at the movement and swallowed back a small bit of bile.

Closing her eyes, she chuckled once more. "Joke's on you, old man. I can barely keep my eyes open. When I do, there's two of you. I'll end up puking all over those clean dishes."

"Cross is getting you some dry crust to gnaw on. It will help your stomach and if you puke, then you just wash what you dirty, plain and simple. That will be payment for a place to sleep."

The crust did help a bit. In fact, as she chewed on the dry bread, she realized this was the first food she'd put in her mouth all day. From there she followed Cross to the back kitchen area and did the dishes, slowly. The whole post was emptied out by the time she was done, miraculously not puking.

She dragged the mop across the floors with as much strength as she could muster. Exhaustion didn't cover it. Her fingers throbbed, the buzz from earlier having almost worn completely off. When she'd gotten about halfway through, Old Beard marched over to her and took the mop. "There's bandages, cleaning alcohol, water and a pill in the hut. Clean your fingers, re-bandage them and take the pill. It will knock you out. Come back and see me tomorrow."

She shook her head in disbelief. "Why do you keep helping me?"

"I knew your father. He was a good friend, though a bit misguided. I knew your mother too and she wasn't always a Zephyr. She came from here, from Argest."

"I didn't know that." The knowledge was like a brick being thrown at her chest. She'd known very little about her mother growing up since her father refused to give her knowledge or comfort for killing the woman he'd loved.

Old Beard patted her shoulder and pushed her gently toward the door. "Go and we'll talk more tomorrow."

She stumbled and slowly made her way to the hut. Throbbing fingers, weak arms, heavy legs…she wanted a cot and to pass out. But her fingers, the bandages were wet, soaked through, and that wasn't good for healing.

Once in the hut, she bolted the door and set about getting herself cleaned up. It was a struggle, but the cleaning solution and the painful sting it brought gave her a burst of energy. When she finally took the pill and lay down ready for oblivion, she welcomed the rest. Though that was when Jack came, when his voice washed over her and she longed for the heat of him or the comfort of his closeness.

"I miss him," she sobbed into the darkness. "I love him."

The words only made her cry more. She reached for a blanket from the other cot, inhaling a little hint of Jack's smell and the scent of sex that still remained.

I love you. Shannon, I care for you with a deep need I don't want and can't stop.

She had to get out of here, find a way to Wespero and to the race stadium. Get back to him and tell him she felt the same. But to do that she had to make changes, be willing to stop destroying herself before she got started.

"In the morning…" She drifted off then to the dream of Jack's smile and once again finding a place in his arms.

Chapter Nineteen

"You told her you loved her and then you left her?" Hemi sat on the couch, holding a full glass. He took a good sip then shrugged his shoulders. "I still don't get it."

Jack had spent the last couple of hours telling Hemi everything that had happened. He left out the details of his and Shannon's sexual encounters but didn't hide that he'd been intimate with her.

"She lied to us, Hemi. To all of us and to me, continuously. She's got Inncukai chasing her at Bridget's command and until she stops trying to live a life full of risks, gambling everything away over and over in the hopes her luck holds... I just can't."

"Can't or won't?" Hemi's question hit Jack square in the gut, a solid punch to his full stomach.

"You don't understand... Necklace aside, she can't..."

Hemi let out a dark chuckle. "Funny, you'd think I don't get it, but I do. Never saw myself with half a cybernetic body at the peak of my racing career. Hell, I married a woman from my past after reuniting with her in less than forty-eight hours, and her father hates me. But here we are. I know all about unmet expectations and how what we've built up in our minds is better than reality. Yet you said it yourself. Despite your best attempts, you fell for a woman who appears to enjoy making the same mistakes your mother did."

"Which I don't want to live through over and over."

"I don't want to be half machine and half man...or married, for that matter. But, if it means a future filled with happiness... Maybe you can't save her from herself and maybe she won't change. Yet, if you set aside all your misgivings and open your heart, she might be willing to try. Even if you had weeks, years with her, wouldn't that be better than sitting here in your lonely-as-fuck little house full of coulds, woulds and shoulds?"

Jack let those words wash over him like a cleansing ion shower. He recalled those moments of happiness Hemi had mentioned. The night at the Trading Post, their last moments together, even their banter amid fights and messes. She'd never abandoned him. *And you left her.*

At the same time... "What if it's not enough?"

"Enough of what, for whom?" Hemi said as he tossed back the rest of the water in his glass. "You keep putting stipulations on everything inside of just being. That's the big difference between you and Shannon. She exists in the universe, flows with it, riding the track and adjusting to the obstacles. The same way we would during a race. Only she's doing it in real time. You're so afraid of what you might lose you won't even jump on the track."

Jack traced his teeth with his tongue, keeping his mouth shut at his objections. He looked down at his cybernetic leg, thinking back to when he'd volunteered for the procedure. How he'd been scared out of his mind, but the promise of walking again was something he couldn't turn away from. The racing accident had cost him his leg, but he couldn't risk losing a chance to walk again.

Since getting his leg back, he'd invested everything into Full Throttle, into the success of their town in the wake of the Smith's mismanagement and the lies told. he'd been falsely believing he'd been taking risks while all along he'd been playing it safe himself, always safe. The same town, the same gang, the same house he'd grown up in. Sticking to his strengths, his driving skills, his speed at the track…

"Maybe you're right, but there's something safe in what you know."

Hemi shrugged. "Says you, sitting alone, while the woman you love might be out there getting hurt, tortured."

Jack shoved out of his seat. "You're one to talk. Married to someone you barely know with enemies for in-laws?"

"Well, I mean…it can't get worse, right? She'll figure out I'm useless soon enough and leave. Until then, guess I'm stuck, but at least I'm not alone."

Alone. Jack had waited years for that necklace to show back up. To be given a chance at a future with someone, and he'd pissed it away. "Fuck, you're right. I'm worse than even the villain in that Warg Bailey story Rune's always spouting about."

"You definitely are running away when you should be running toward. Want me to let Drag and Snapper know the test run will be delayed?"

Jack grinned. "Yeah, hate that…just when I got back and I'm healthy."

He felt a little guilty, even more so that if he left and things went wrong, he'd put the rest of his brothers in a lurch. "Before I take off, I need your help."

An hour later the sun was just starting to rise, twinges of light on the horizon. Jack threw his duffle into the side seat of the hauler. The second one he'd be leaving with. Snapper would kill him if he didn't bring this one back.

Hemi held a vial of his blood up in the air, examining it. "This is the stuff, huh?"

"Protect it with your life and get it to Gina this morning. At the very least there should be enough there for her to replicate the second-gen nanites to keep the rest of you running."

"You're coming back. Quit talking like this is the last time I'll see you."

Jack shook his head. "Can't be sure of that, but I'll do my best to get Shannon and return before the race."

If not…well, he couldn't let his head fill with the guilt that would come chasing those thoughts. He needed his focus and concern on the woman he loved and getting her out of Auster territory. The threat of Bridget and her hired assassin would be dealt with when he got Shannon back here to Frog Lick. He'd drop at Drag's feet and promise anything for their leader to help Jack find a solution that kept her alive.

"Let's be optimistic. I think my accident after the win is enough excitement, don't you?" Hemi said, clutching the vial in his human hand.

"Fine, positive thoughts. See you in the morning then." Jack gave a nod, fired up the hauler and tore out of town. He caught Drag on his porch, smoking from a cigar, an eyebrow raised as Jack streaked by, but he didn't bother to stop and share the plan.

No time.

The travel across the Wespero territory back to the checkpoint at Auster was filled with contemplation, plans, ideas for the future, words of possible forgiveness he could offer Shannon for being an idiot and leaving her.

Hemi had been right. Jack kept letting the past scare him into not taking action for the future. Regardless of the insanity of his trip with Shannon into Auster, there were elements of the experience he'd enjoyed. The exploration and new adventures weren't lost on him either, though he'd been injured because of his leg and unable to act in a helpful capacity.

She'd also proven she'd stick by him no matter what, and he'd done the opposite.

I've got a lot to make up for.

Jack had allowed the necklace and his personal beliefs regarding the talisman to blind him from the reality that he loved Shannon. Love should trump everything, and he'd prove it moving forward.

The checkpoint was within his sights by midday. Maybe she'd already made it this far, and maybe not. Regardless, he'd question the folks here then continue into Auster and find Shannon. If he had no luck, then he'd continue to Argest and Old Beard. There was still some time before the ultimatum Bridget's Inncukai had issued was up.

He brought the hauler to a stop a good half a mile away. The building in the distance shimmered a bit from the heat refracting from the ground. Jack decided to hide the hauler behind a rock formation and make his way in on foot, in case any of those men recognized him. Though he hadn't been stopped on his way back to Frog Lick before, he needed to play the situation smart and with caution.

Walking in, he noticed a couple other vehicles, riders, a hauler or two. There was a fairly good crowd here. Entering through the front door, he took in the small bar to his left, the tables and chairs filled with men, women…some playing games and others draping over a player as if offering them luck.

The set up was similar to Trading Post and the Skeiron gaming hall, but ultimately smaller.

"Stranger, what brings you to the Auster-Wespero border?" This came from a long-haired man with a half-hearted grin.

"Looking for a canteen refill and maybe a crock of whatever the special is."

Jack hoped he was right and they served food. In Wespero, all gang-towns had a public house like the Watering Hole of Frog Lick where food, drink, music and gathering were encouraged. Auster seemed focused on games of chance and skill everywhere anyone went. The challenge for risk was so prevalent in life he should have realized sooner that his mother's obsession was born of a childhood love for where she'd come from.

"Eh, we got a bone broth…best I can offer. Substance, outside of some space bread, is kind of hard to find."

Space bread? Jack hadn't heard of that before. "Broth is fine. It'll be a taste different than water. I'll take it."

He slid half a leaf onto the bar top, along with slapping his canteen within reach of the bartender.

Long-hair snatched up both with a quick glance. "I'll be right back."

"Wait?" Better time than never. "Has a woman with thick, dark, curly hair passed through here in the last day or so?"

Long-hair lowered his chin and shook his hair out of his eyes. "What's this woman to you?"

"She's mine." The words were firm and sudden. Jack had never intended to say such a thing out loud, but making the claim was right in these circumstances. Often the idiots in other gang-towns only saw women as property...a stupid and antiquated belief that he and those in Full Throttle wanted to erase.

"Is that right?" a low voice said from behind him.

Jack began to pivot, fists raised because the voice was one he'd heard before at the Trading Post. But something crashed against the back of his head before he even caught sight of the other person. Jack fell to his knees, eyelids heavy, the back of his head throbbing, and all he could see in front of him was black fabric swirling. Then he fell asleep.

* * * *

Shannon's feet ached. Her face itched from the cloth she'd used to cover herself from the sun, which was now setting. The checkpoint at the border of Wespero and Auster lay in the distance and she'd make it before dark.

"Un-fucking-believable."

Because she'd been walking for a week. No amount of labor that she'd given Old Beard had resulted in him attempting to help her find a ride. He'd been as bad as Jack encouraging her to quit looking to her old practices to dig herself out of the hole she'd been left in.

After two more days of putting up with the bastard, winning a little crinkle in some games that Cross had stupidly agreed to play her in—no doubt because he liked her—she'd set off on her own across the barren terrain.

Traveling sunup to sundown and barely sleeping for fear a slither would find her, she traversed Auster for a week—feet only moved so fast. She'd been lucky Old Beard had given her two full canteens and food, along with a covering to keep her skin from burning under the sun.

She was thankful for her supplies as the days wore on, and only the constant replay of Jack's words, how he'd confessed his love, kept her moving. She'd find a way to show him, but first she had to get to Wespero.

Of course, the problem with Bridget still remained, but maybe the flash... *Who are you kidding?*

No way would Bridget call off her Inncukai without the plans to the racer and Shannon wasn't in a position to get those. She wouldn't anyway because that was a bullshit ask.

Her resolve even firmer, she marched into the checkpoint ready to do whatever she needed to get a ride to Frog Lick. Someone inside had to help her. Maybe for a canteen...something.

The place happily didn't hold the men she'd gotten into a disagreement with last time, but as she unwound her head wrap, the bartender called out to her.

"You, dark and curly hair... Come here." He was long-haired and scruffy with a lazy eye, and much leaner than the previous barkeep she'd met.

"Can I help you?" She was hesitant in her steps, fearing a trap.

"There was a message left for you. Said to give it to you whenever you showed up."

"Me?" Shannon pointed at herself and looked around the room. The tables were mostly empty, a couple men argued with each other over cards.

"Yeah, you...female, short, with dark, curly hair. I don't got anything other than this scrap of paper. Who uses paper anymore?" The bartender flipped a piece of tan parchment onto the bar.

"Who's it from?"

Bartender shrugged. "Said they were a friend."

Jack... She crossed the room in a hurry, snatching up that piece of paper like a precious heirloom. The first words she'd heard from him. Maybe he'd realized his mistake. *Maybe...* All good thoughts melted away at the words as she scanned them.

The unmistakable *B* was signed at the bottom, with the little flourish. The same one Bridget had added to everyone in Macintosh tattoo brand. Except Bridget got off on applying that B to the gang tat herself with a heated poker instead of ink.

We have Jack, and we're not giving him back until I see those racer plans. Bring them within the week or we start cutting his fingers off...

The bitch.

"When was she here? When did they take him?" For all Shannon knew, this was a lie and a trap. Wouldn't take much to figure out he'd been traveling with her, but he'd booked it for Frog Lick.

"About eight days ago."

Fuck... "They say they have my friend. Did a man come in here looking for me?"

Lazy Eye nodded. "Yep, same day the woman with this note arrived. He asked me for water and to know if I'd seen a woman with dark, curly hair. But you hadn't shown up yet. He was tall, short-cropped hair, a good amount of scruff...a dark blond."

"Blue eyes and good muscle tone?"

"What the hell you take me for?" Lazy Eye gave her scowl. "I'm not commenting on his looks, but he's bigger than me, okay?"

Jack. Shit, and she took him.

Shannon crumpled the note from Bridget in her fist. "How much for a cycler, a hauler...anything that can get me into Wespero faster than my own two feet?"

"I don't have nothing like that. No visitors for days, and those two fools over there wouldn't trade you their ride for anything. They're couriers for a couple of Auster gangs—they'd shoot before they took you anywhere. Always waiting for their next gig."

She sighed. "My feet it is then. Fill the canteen?"

When two canteens came back to her, she frowned. "What's this for?"

"The one is your friend's. He paid for the water, but never got to take it with him. Good luck, lady. Hope you get him back."

Out of the door she went, first walking, then running. The sun was setting but she had no choice. She had to keep moving, into Wespero territory and toward...*dust honeys and klogs.*

Did she go to Bridget and offer her own life in return for freeing Jack? Or did she go to Frog Lick and try to get Drag and the others to help?

211

Both options came with plenty of risks. As she ran, a glimmer caught her eye to the right. She slowed, walking around a boulder, and there it sat. A Frog Lick, Full Throttle hauler, evidenced by the marker on the hood.

When she hopped into the hauler, she quickly pressed a button and the engine powered right up. Didn't take long to get pointed on the path to Frog Lick. She was prepared to grovel to Drag and the others, to even be honest about what happened if they promised to help.

She dismissed the idea of going straight to Macintosh because no way would Bridget let Jack go for a bodily trade. The leader was too vindictive and hated when people didn't follow through on her bidding. Shannon would probably be killed on the spot, then Bridget would use Jack.

Jack… The idea of him being tortured because of her cut so deep. *A murderer.* If he died, she really would be. She revved up the hauler and increased speed.

No way would he die. *Not if I can help it.*

Which was why she drove straight to the mechanics bay when getting into Frog Lick. Though instead of finding Drag, she found the whole group.

Hemi was the one to see her first and he nudged Drag. All eyes were on her as she stood awkwardly right inside the mechanics bay doors.

"Where's Jack?" Snapper hollered at her.

"He's been taken."

Chapter Twenty

Shannon was prepared for Jack's friends to look at her with hatred, to hit her or throw things. This was the way her own people had treated her for years and how she'd even been viewed by the moonies after being part of Kascade's organization.

Instead, Gina charged toward her. As she approached, Shannon prepared for a slap, a hit, but not...a hug. Gina wrapped her arms around Shannon and pulled her close.

"Are you okay?" the woman whispered in her ear.

Shannon couldn't stop the tears welling in her eyes. "I'm fine, but Jack... Bridget took him."

Gina didn't release her, just patted her back, offering comfort. "We thought something went wrong when he didn't return with you. We've been discussing options. Now you're here and we have answers. You must have been frightened."

Shannon stiffened up at those words. "I'm not frightened. I'm angry and I want to get Jack back. He shouldn't have to pay for my mistakes."

Gina pulled away first and looked at her, then the blonde mechanic released her and stepped back. "You love him?"

"What's that got to do with it?" Snapper said, marching toward them. "Bridget's crazy. He could already be dead."

"No," Drag replied. "She wouldn't kill him. That would guarantee she'd never get what she wants."

The leader of Full Throttle eyed Shannon as the rest of them shared looks of confusion.

"What does she want?" Hemi asked.

Shannon sighed and linked her hands together. "The plans to your racer. She purposely cheated in a game of cards against me, so I'd be in her debt. The explosion in Hemi's racer wasn't an accident. At least I don't think it was, because she waited to claim what I owed her until I was contacted by Gina's friend on the moonie base. I don't know what she has against you all, but she's bound and determined to defeat you at any cost."

Snapper shared a look with Drag, but Shannon refused to inquire more. She didn't care about their squabbles. She cared about getting Jack back, giving him a chance at a future. Hopefully, one where he'd be with her.

She shook at the thought, physically vibrating at knowing how bad she wanted to have his arms around her again. To even have him frown at her poor decisions. Hell, she'd do stupid things to get him to look at her.

"Whatever her reasons, I don't really give a shit. But I'm willing to do whatever to get Jack back. If it was as simple as trading myself for him, I would. Though I'm afraid she won't accept that as a decent trade anymore."

"No, she won't. Bridget has committed to kidnapping one of ours instead of using an outside source. Are you sure it was her?"

Shannon tugged the crumpled letter out of her pocket and shoved her fist toward Drag. He walked over to her and picked the ball carefully from her hand with his cybernetic one. Unfolding the letter, Drag's eyes traced the words and Shannon watched as the frown on his face deepened, a sharp indent above his left eye as his gaze narrowed. He shoved the letter at Snapper, who let out a string of curse words after he read the contents.

"We go after him." Drag's declaration was met with Snapper and Hemi's agreements.

"For more than one reason," Gina replied. "The blood Jack left wasn't enough. I can't replicate the nanites without more, unfortunately. If we leave out our emotional attachments to him, he's still needed to ensure the rest of you with cybernetics survive."

Shannon frowned and crossed her arms. "He has to be worth more than blood to you."

Gina waved away her concern. "Yes, he is. Still, it bears mentioning we need to bring him back alive and intact."

A bang, heavy and resounding, could be heard against the main bay doors. Then it repeated twice more, which sent a fresh wave of fear through her.

Snapper went to answer it. His booming voice barked out a muffled greeting of some sort. When he returned, his face was flustered, his cybernetic hand clenched tight while the other one held a cloth. "You're right, she's desperate."

He handed over the cloth and a small card to Drag, who peeled back the stained linen to reveal a small finger, darkened and decaying.

"This is your first present, two more days and I'll send another," Drag read aloud before crumpling the card up in his hand and tossing it. "She's determined to take pieces from all of us... I'm not letting her get another one."

Shannon stared at the pinky and put a fist against her mouth to keep herself from screaming. He'd been hurt because of her...even as he'd left her to her own devices, to solve her own issues, he still got caught up in them. "We have to call someone. The protectorate, the commission...someone can stop her."

Hemi scoffed. "You know better. Protectorate cares only if the commission is threatened. Commission don't care unless a gang is breaking the rules of the charters. Kidnapping some woman's man and holding him hostage until she pays her debts is perfectly legal in their eyes."

Shannon knew that, but hated it all the same. The fact no one would step in against this madwoman and her stupid schemes was ridiculous. If they couldn't get outside help, then Jack's rescue fell back onto her.

"So, I guess it's best that I go alone." Shannon refused to endanger anyone else that Jack cared about. "What I'm looking at you for is a bargaining chip. Give me something, even a fake something... I need to go to Bridget with some sort of plan in place."

"You're not going by yourself. That's not how we work." Drag had covered Jack's pinky back up and set it to the side.

"I can't possibly risk harm coming to anyone Jack loves." She'd be devastated if she brought him more pain than she already had. He'd seen her, all of her, and still loved her. He'd even been coming to get her. *Shit*.

Hemi put a hand on her shoulder. "But you're the one Jack cared about the most. Nothing bad can happen to you, either. Ultimately, Full Throttle's involvement is not your decision to make. We can decide how we want to proceed."

Tears gathered at her eyes again and Shannon blinked them away. She refused to cry any more at their kindness or at the realization Jack had tried to return for her. The others started to voice their agreement or opinions.

Then Gina's surprising giggle brought silence to the room. The blonde woman had a knuckle in her mouth and was staring at the floor.

"Care to share, love?" Snapper asked.

Gina lifted her head, a wide grin on her face. "I have an idea, but it will still be dangerous. If Bridget really has assassins and bullies on her side, any plan could result in someone getting hurt."

"As long as it's not Jack, I'm good." Shannon fingered the necklace, then gripped the charm in her palm. *It's not a curse.*

No, this necklace…her faith in it had kept her alive all these years. She'd channel that into hope and the belief she could save him.

"All right, then this is what we'll do…" Gina started to elaborate, and Shannon hunkered down, trying her best to pay attention.

Regardless of whatever they came up with, she'd learned today that Jack was right. Telling the truth got her further than hiding behind lies. These people surrounding her could have offered her nothing but hate. Instead, they were willing to take her help and give in return.

"You get that, Shannon...you'll be the target."

She nodded. "I'm good with that."

Anything for Jack... *Anything to save him.*

* * * *

Jack blinked awake, aware of an aching pain in his hand that refused to go away. With each passing second as he came to, the pain increased, a searing agony as if he'd burned himself badly. The scent of scorched flesh lingered in the air.

"What the hell happened?"

"Your woman never showed, so I made good on my threat." A smooth velvet voice washed over him. Jack gave a little shiver as the woman speaking came into view.

She was beautiful, of course — long red tresses piled high on her head, a tan vest covering an off-white blouse that accentuated her breasts. Her curves were clearly lined too, an enticing package meant to draw the eye and make men or women lose their minds. Of that Jack had no doubt, but her looks were it, because when their gazes met, his appreciation withered. Those green depths held the look of a woman who was dead inside. No emotion reflected back at him.

"You're Bridget."

She laughed, a little half-hearted two syllable sound. "How did you guess?"

"Red hair, heartless gaze...kind of hard to match that up with anyone else. I've heard plenty of stories."

The amusement on her face disappeared in an instant. "Well then, I hope I live up to them. Your pinky has been sent off to Full Throttle. I'm happy to say I've claimed a piece of each one of you cybernetic idiots, one way or another."

Jack schooled his features. "Bragging isn't a trait most people enjoy."

"Neither is weakness, but you and your Full Throttle family love to embrace frailty. According to my spies, Shannon will arrive today. Now the question is if your friends are going to destroy her before I get the pleasure, or has she done more damage attempting to get me what she promised?"

Jack lifted his hand and looked at the burnt, mottled flesh that rested in the spot where his left pinky had once been. "Debts aren't promises."

"Aren't they?" Bridget motioned to Jack. "Come sit with me over at this table. I've kept you untied, but try anything and the Inncukai you can't see will end you before you get out of the door."

The room itself was awash in low light. There were layers and layers of sheet drapes in a variety of reds, purples and blues hanging from the ceiling, making it hard to tell who was in the room or where anyone was.

"Where am I?" Jack asked as he slowly stood up. He used his right hand to brace himself against the chair for leverage because the left still stupidly believed there were five fingers there.

For the last several days he'd been kept in some sort of storage hut, surrounded by dirt wood bits. They'd shoved swill and stale food cubes at him. No violence, until the day prior when the Inncukai that had hurt Shannon had come for his finger. He'd been helpless against the mercenaries graceful and debilitating moves. For that moment, he'd been able to relate to how Shannon must have felt.

Bridget chuckled. "You honestly don't even have a good guess? I thought the members of Full Throttle were smarter. Though I guess not, since none of you detected that bomb we placed in your racer."

The truth was now doubly confirmed. This woman was to blame for what had happened to Hemi. He wasn't the only person she'd hurt. No, Jack personally was aware of how she'd hurt Drag and Rune, and would have killed Petal if allowed. Even Snapper had cause to despise her. She got off on hurting people, especially people he cared for.

"Maybe you'd like to help her out and play Judas, instead?"

Who the hell is Judas? Jack made a fist and his nerve endings raged anew in pain as he collapsed into the chair Bridget had pulled out for him. An octagon-shaped table was in front of him, covered in fitted, soft cloth. The Macintosh symbol was etched in gold in the center of the table, the intertwined knot with the unmistakable M in the center. Though near the bottom a symbolic B had been carved into the table, showing through the cloth.

"Silent, huh? Fine...you can listen then." Bridget sat down in the seat next to him in an inelegant manner, spreading her clad legs wide and propping her head up on one palm. "Your gang is run by a hypocrite. One who has obviously never shared the stories passed down about the Macintosh, who first colonized the Wespero region, and all others who were late arrivals. We're a bit more enlightened than other gangs—"

"A bit more insane," Jack replied.

With lightning speed, Bridget lashed out with a strike. Her hand moved so swift he didn't expect the heavy sting she laid against his cheek with the slap.

"You're too much like him."

Light flooded the room as the door opened with squeaky hinges. "Ma'am, we've got a hauler incoming. Shannon is on it."

"Ah." Bridget sat up straight and tugged at the sleeves of her shirt, the three-quarter length coming right past her elbows. "Appears you might be spared after all. Escort her in once she arrives and do the usual."

Jack arched a brow. "I did hear stories, but none of them really conveyed how paranoid you are."

"That's preparedness, you mean? Paranoia is for those who act out of constant fear. I do what I do based on awareness. You've seen what I'm capable of, and even if Drag is stupid, I at least respect the fact my abilities can be replicated."

This woman was delusional about a lot of things, but at least she didn't appear to underestimate Full Throttle. He wondered what they'd said to Shannon, what she felt. Had she traveled to Frog Lick and survived?

The door squeaked open again.

"…Unbelievable, all the trouble I went through thanks to Bridget kidnapping…" Shannon glanced toward them, though those damn sheer hanging curtains kept a good view of her somewhat obscured. He saw her shake her arm to get her escort to let her go. Jack now realized why Bridget used the curtains — as a distraction and possible confusion if anyone tried to attack her.

She stomped toward them, words still flying. "You should have just given me more time, left Jack alone. Now you can't claim any deniability in this. Drag and Full Throttle know you're after them."

Shannon brushed aside the sheer curtains, coming closer. Jack realized he was holding his breath, waiting to see her, like he was waiting for food or water. He'd been so desperate to have her face in his sight again.

The last curtain moved and slowly he exhaled as her visage became clear. Her curls were pulled back out of her face by a strip of cloth, and the top she wore was a V-neck shirt with the necklace he'd made clearly visible. He wanted to believe that was a sign, but couldn't tell from her gaze, wholly focused on Bridget, if she cared about him.

"Who gives a shit? If my goals are achieved, that's what mattered. Did you get them?"

Shannon glanced at him only a quick second, and Jack could have sworn the bravado she displayed was part of her ongoing act. He'd seen the cocky way she stood, the arch of her back, and the point of her chin whenever she challenged someone.

She replicated the same stance now as Bridget inquired again, "Where are the plans?"

Shannon frowned and pulled something small out of her pants pocket. "Right here. You're lucky they didn't kill me on the spot."

"Hmm, I mean if they did, I would still have had Jack here as a bargaining chip." Bridget snatched the little file drive Shannon held from her outstretched hand and immediately stood up. "Wait here while I check those. Remember there are eyes on you. So don't try anything."

As Bridget marched away, the curtains falling back in place behind her disappearing form, Shannon came to Jack's side.

"How are you here?" Jack mused aloud, still baffled by this turn of events. He'd rebuked her, pushed her away. Hell, he hadn't even begged for forgiveness yet.

"Don't worry about that. Is the finger the only body part they took?"

Jack nodded, as he held out his hands to display the damage. "Nothing worth missing."

She crouched in front of him and took his hands into hers, as she gently examined the damage to his left one. "All hell's about to break loose. When I give the word, follow me," she whispered.

A moment's trepidation rushed through him. He wanted to ask about the Inncukai, the threat Bridget held over their heads of an assassin who had hurt Shannon already and had no restraint about violence and murder.

Then the room plunged into darkness. Shannon tugged on his hands. "Let's go."

Chapter Twenty-One

Jack came with little resistance, something Shannon was thankful for. She wanted to kill Bridget and the Inncukai, who was no doubt the one who had actually cut off Jack's finger. But revenge wasn't on the agenda — rescuing Jack was.

With a good idea of the direction of the door, Shannon hunched low and hoped Jack stayed in tune with her as they made their escape, silently praying the Full Throttle crew followed through on their word. The Inncukai was still a concern for Shannon, but Gina had repeatedly stated not to worry about the assassin.

They passed the curtains and made it to the main part of the floor, where the door was in sight. Footsteps scrambled around them. Bridget's shrill voice issued commands. "Secure the prisoners. Where's my assassin? What do you mean no longer at their post?"

The other words, from whoever was speaking, were too low to make out, but they needed to move quickly.

"Secure the exits if they aren't at the table. And don't fire inside — we won't…turn the lamps."

Light started to illuminate the area in front of them. Only a couple feet from the door, but the lamps would make them targets.

Shannon stood up and Jack stumbled a bit as he tried to follow her move. She tried her best to stabilize herself against his strength so they both didn't end up face first.

A single shot fired, and she briefly squeezed her eyes shut, preparing for the pain to hit her or a groan to come from Jack. When nothing happened, she was ready to move.

"Run!" She let go of Jack's hand and beelined for the exit. They had to get out that door then a ride would be waiting.

Better be there.

Her heart pounded in her chest, her ears. She could barely make sense of anything besides the fact she wanted to survive and wanted Jack with her. Another shot rang out and she ignored it, shoving her whole body against the door and willing with every fiber of her being it would open. When it did, she couldn't stop the surprised, "Oh!" that burst from her mouth.

Jack barreled into her. They were a tangle of arms, brushed torsos and fumbling legs as they stumbled into the late afternoon sky. They both finally got upright and to a stop. Jack's uninjured hand fisted in her hair, his other at her waist.

"You came for me," he said in a low voice that melted into her skin.

"Of course…I love you."

The sun was already moving past some of the buildings behind them, the low light setting a mood, sparking arousal amid danger. She should get her head checked out, but this hit all her high-risk preferred tendencies.

"You two care to save the declarations and smooching for when we're out of danger and get in the damn hauler!" Drag's voice cleared away her momentary lust and she stepped out of Jack's embrace.

He frowned for a split second, then scooped her up against his body and carried her the rest of the way. She almost yelled at him to put her down, but the look of determination and devotion in his eyes, and the strength in his grip, kept her silent. Jack wrenched open the door to the hauler.

Only then did he set her down. She winked at him. "Your leg is feeling good, then?"

He smiled. "Get in the damn hauler."

She hopped into the back seat and strapped a safety belt over her lap. The door to the building Jack had been held in burst open and Bridget stepped out. Her previously coiffed hairdo was in shambles, a smudge of dirt on her cheek. She had a gun trained on them.

"I'll fucking shoot you all if you move. I'm a dead shot, won every quick-draw contest. You can ask your fearless leader."

Drag's loud obnoxious laugh echoed around her as he leaned back in the driver's seat. "I'd love to see you try. My experience with you is that you'd rather someone else actually pull the trigger."

"Oh, dare me do you?" She cocked the hammer back.

"Bridget, you're so desperate, you've resorted to pointing guns at people. When you know damn well I like to fight other ways." Drag winked at her and she pointed the gun at him this time. Before she could pull the trigger, an explosion rocked the ground. Flames erupted from the building they'd come from, then smoke.

"We're out of here, folks." Drag took off as a second explosion shook the vehicle. "Might need to tell Snapper and Gina to dial it back a bit next time."

"Snapper? Gina?" Jack glanced back at her. "Why did you haul everyone into this?"

"Me?" Shannon pointed at herself. "I didn't have a choice in the matter. I was willing to turn myself over to Bridget, give my life up in exchange for yours. They wouldn't let me. Outright refusal. They wouldn't even hate me."

"I don't hate you." He repositioned himself in the seat and held out his hand.

She put her hand in his and he squeezed gently. "And I don't hate you. I said some things."

He shook his head. "Stop... Just give me a minute. I was coming back for you. I realized I had some expectations and issues I was forcing onto you. You're great and maybe a risk now and then isn't so horrible."

"Just tell her you're sorry." Drag gripped the steering wheel tighter as they raced across the terrain, the sun reflecting off the horizon in front of them. "Apologizing is far better than excuses."

"And you would know how to deal with women, Drag? Your last romantic entanglement was going to shoot you."

Shannon giggled. "Wait...him and Bridget?"

"Let's stop talking about me and you two figure this shit out before we get back to Frog Lick. Do you love each other?"

Jack stared at her. His gaze still held the devotion she'd witnessed earlier. Totally different from how he'd looked at her when he'd walked away at the Trading Post. "Yeah, I love her. I want to make you an offer if you're willing."

"Talk boring to me," Shannon replied, scooting to the edge of the seat as best she could.

"My house, we share it. You stay in Frog Lick and from time to time we venture out. Visit other gang-towns, learn more about the people around us. Spread a friendly word."

Drag groaned. "We don't need friendly words."

"We do if we're going to war with Macintosh, which is what you just did."

Shannon stroked Jack's cheek, loving the scruffiness from his unshaved face. "They said the commission won't do anything—"

"It's the lack of interference we need to worry about," Jack said as he turned to press a kiss to her fingers. "But...never mind that, back to us. A together cohabitation where we're in it for the long haul. I can't promise we won't fight or disagree. But I'll promise to do my darndest to give you the best sex you ever had."

Shannon laughed. "I'd be a fool to say no then."

"Seriously?" Drag asked. "All he has to promise you is sex?"

"No...I expect a lot more than that. But I know he'll give it to me. He jacked this heart a long time ago."

Jack grinned and kissed the back of her hand, nodding at the necklace. "I'm glad you kept it."

"I won't ever take it off. It brought me the most important thing in my life. You."

"Get a room." Drag groaned as they continued their journey.

"That's the plan, as soon as we get back."

Chapter Twenty-Two

"I don't need a cybernetic pinky finger." Jack slammed his empty mug on the table and wiped his chin.

"But you could have one." Shannon was relentless, always, and he'd never been happier since returning to Frog Lick. Sure, the fact they were officially in a gang war with Macintosh didn't ease anyone's minds. In fact, there was a subtle discontent among the gang members, especially when Drag announced Jack wouldn't race for the next regional.

With his new injury and the championship race only a month away, the commission doctor had ruled him ineligible. All the residents were worried and feared they'd lose the chance at the championship.

"It's a dumb decision," Gaia said, coming over to their table with fresh mugs.

"Not to have a cyborg pinky, I agree." Shannon had been bringing it up for days.

"No, not letting Jack race. He could have gloved up and been completely safe. A pinky doesn't affect the ability to put the pedal down and burn tire on the track."

Shannon looked down at her new drink and kept silent. She'd been happy Jack wasn't racing, voicing her concerns plenty loud to Drag and the others in their small circle that she feared Macintosh attempting to blow up their racer again. They were all living in a state of heightened concern, unsure when Bridget would attempt to attack them next.

"Yes," Drag replied, joining them at the table. "But then it takes away Hemi's chance to really show his skills. He's recovering well thanks to Shannon's work and the help they brought back from Auster. Plus, he needs to do something to impress his in-laws if he plans to keep that wife."

Gaia scoffed. "Never thought I'd see the day when anyone from Auster gave anything to anyone other than themselves, or see Hemi married."

"Today's that day." Shannon raised her glass in the air. "To Auster and Hemi."

Jack followed, along with Drag. Even Gaia mumbled the toast before she turned and walked off. Drag waited until she'd gone completely back to the bar before pulling up a chair.

"Any word?" Jack asked. He'd been worried since they'd escaped. Had nightmares that were staved off by Shannon's warm body and her willingness to do anything to distract him.

Drag scooted in. "Nothing new. Gina's plan worked. The virus she put in that card you passed to Bridget gave us a backdoor into their systems. But Gina's not as fast as she once was. It's taking a little longer to comb through the information she downloaded. Bridget isn't stupid. She's already shut us out of the system."

"Then we wait. We play it safe," Shannon offered, finishing off her drink. "While we do that, I'm taking this one home."

Jack reached out for Shannon's hand, loving how she tried to distract from the possibilities. How she reminded Jack constantly to not worry about the future and focus on the present. "Afraid I have to agree with her. We'll stick with the plan. Keep our racer safe, get Hemi up to par and go for the championship. I'm sure Bridget will eventually pop up with a new scheme."

"But for now, we enjoy life?" Drag chuckled. "Get on with it, you two."

Jack stood up and pulled Shannon with him. "Don't have to tell us twice."

They were both grinning like idiots as they left the Watering Hole behind and headed for his place…no, their place. Shannon had put her magic touch on the home he'd once shared with his parents. He welcomed her touches of color and the life breathed back into a space he'd begun to believe trapped him in the past.

"Are you worried about Bridget?" Shannon asked as they reached their front door.

"I'm more concerned about anything happening to you." Which was the truth. Jack had wanted Shannon to feel like she belonged here, because what mattered to him most was being a part of her life.

"Nothing will happen to me. As long as I stay with you…I'll do whatever I can to help Full Throttle." She'd been saying that ever since they came back to Frog Lick. Repeating the phrase almost every day, as if the more she said it, the more it made her conviction true. But

Jack viewed her actions as more enticing than her words.

"You're not honor-bound to do anything. You helped free me, you got us the nanites to save my brothers. It's all about us now…quit worrying about Full Throttle. One way or another, the gang and the town will survive. We're too stubborn not to."

"Yeah, but I brought more attention to you all, caused you to go directly for Bridget."

Jack shrugged as he opened the door to their place. "It would have happened eventually. Bridget was already working against us, evidenced by her forcing you to attempt to steal from us. The bonus is we confirmed she was responsible for the accident that hurt Hemi."

Shannon walked in first then turned to face him, moving backward. "Fine, I'll concede. Enough worrying, talking about the coming war. Let's talk about something even more important."

Jack shut the door and leaned against it as he secured the lock. "What's that?"

"Us."

Shannon had done her best over the last month to try to show her redemption. How she was done with unnecessary risks, unless Jack was willing to take a chance right along with her. She'd coaxed him into gambling with her in one of the card games they held periodically at the Watering Hole. He'd raced with her on a hauler under a midnight sky, the moons bright and clear.

He'd even had sex with her on top of the mechanics bay at night, allowing them to be loud and crude and not giving a fuck who heard them. Jack had proved by far he wanted to be her partner in all things, and she'd been so grateful. It was insane how he'd taken her back after that fateful day at Bridget's, even if her decision had sent them into a war Full Throttle didn't deserve.

"You know I love you, right?" she asked as Jack started up the heating element in the main room, his back to her, crouched down on the balls of his feet. "I mean…I haven't said it that much."

He stood up slowly, still facing away from her, and a little bit of fear crept into her gut. What if he didn't…nope, he professed his love to her every which way. From morning breakfast and beverage to the little notes he'd tuck into her pants pocket to find when she went off to work with Hemi on physical therapy. Then dinner. No matter what, he made sure she was cared for, cherished.

"Jack, I…" She walked toward him and tugged on his arm.

He turned willingly, then she saw the tears tracking down his cheeks.

She couldn't help but reach for him, using her thumbs to wipe away the moisture. "Jack—"

"Men aren't supposed to cry, I know. We're supposed to be tough, not weak."

She shook her head. "No, who the fuck says that? Tears don't make you weak. They mean you have feelings. You're human and you have a soul. You care. Just tell me if I did something wrong."

"No." He wrapped her hands up in his, pulling them down and away from his face. "You did everything right. You love me. That's a gift I've wanted since the moment I realized you were the one. The necklace…hell, maybe before that. Someone to love me as me. Someone to appreciate—"

She cut him off with a kiss, leaning up on her tiptoes and smashing her lips against his. "You're perfect…every inch of you," she mumbled against him. Then he was kissing her back. Letting her hands go, he scooped her into his arms, hoisting her up by her thighs. They were moving fast and she didn't care.

Shannon just focused on kissing him, letting their tongues greet each other like long-lost lovers. The connection turned insistent, until she nipped him with her teeth. She wanted him all the ways, but her favorite was when he went completely wild.

Except he held her off, refusing to bite back as he got them into the bedroom then gently set her down.

"You can throw me, ya know. I won't break."

He booped her on the nose then pressed a kiss there as he went to his knees. "Normally, I would, but instead of fucking you senseless, I want to worship you tonight."

She let him pull her pants off and spread her thighs, loving the way he pressed kisses up each leg. "You have too many clothes on."

"Then I'll take them off." Jack stood and began to strip.

Instead of watching him, Shannon quickly rid herself of the rest of her clothes. Jack's gaze on her was like that of a starving man, ravenous and greedy. He climbed onto the bed and returned to his place between her legs, giving attention to her breasts as well.

"You want my tongue on your pussy?"

She moaned.

"That's not yes… Tell me how you want me to lick you until you cream all over my face?"

Shannon giggled. "You really want that?"

"I love to see you free from inhibition," he replied with a grin. "The way you look, the pleasure you experience."

Shannon caressed his cheek before pushing his head back down. "A little more action then. Show me how you like to eat me 'til I explode."

Jack got to work, licking at her like he was feasting upon the last meal of his life, judging from the appreciative groans he made.

She basked in his adoration, gripping his hair in her hands and guiding him in his ministrations. Nothing aroused her more than this sight of him playing supplicant to her, that he loved her in this way. He was dedicated to ensuring her happiness and she only hoped she could do the same. That the depth of her admiration and love for him would equal his.

"You're thinking too much and that means I'm not doing my job very well," Jack said in between his attentions.

"No, admiring you."

Jack grinned and went back to it. His renewed efforts wiped away rational thoughts, as he began to tweak and fondle her breasts. Before long she was panting and desperate, near begging him to put his tongue to the very spot she needed.

"I'm going to—" Her release hit, cutting her off as she not only found her orgasm but covered Jack in it.

He climbed up the rest of the way, covering her body with his, then sank in deep.

"Yesssss," she hissed, loving the way he filled her up. His movements were slow strokes, giving way to a fast pace as he sought to bring her to a second orgasm. This was what she wanted, her nails digging into his back, the moans of satisfaction as he started to tense and stretch over her. They were rutting animals and she would lust after this type of connection with him until the end of her days.

He shouted her name, then clasped her tightly to him as he rolled to his side. "I love you," he murmured.

"And I love you…Jack." She pressed her lips to his, loving the taste of her on him.

They would conquer the future together, hearts entwined and ready for whatever the ride might bring.

Glossary

Airponics: Indoor greenhouse.

Barnabas: Affiliated Wespero territory gang-town.

BCS: Body Collection Service. An organization founded by the Allied Planetary Union that collects dead bodies for bone harvesting.

Bob-tailed scratcher: Possum-type animal with claws and bobbed tail.

Bone powder: Used to power the slip drive by mixing with water. Made from human bones. Most potent when mixed with urine as the acid mixes with the carbon molecules that light up more with electricity.

Bootleggers: Smugglers who run illegal booze from Earth to other planets.

Bumdum: Slang term for bummer.

Coon cat: A striped feral cat with a bushy tail.

Crinkle: Slang term for money.

Dust honey: Slang term for an attractive woman who lives on Mars and hangs around guys or gals in the hopes of gaining attention, money or notoriety.

Fatch: Alternative to the word fuck, in regional use by those from the Upper planets. Used alone or as a noun or verb in various phrases to express annoyance, contempt or impatience.

Flash: Slang term for money.

Fur-buns: Rabbit-type animal that lives in the wilds of Mars.

Gold leaves: Monetary currency, pressed gold in sheets as thin as leaves. Folks call it crinkle or flash depending on who they are and where they're from.

Goosemert: Mouse-like animal that burrows and lets out a honking wail.

Grav boots: Boots with a gravity lock built into the soles, designed for those who travel in space and may need to spacewalk.

Haulers: Four-seater coverless vehicles with a bed attached for hauling supplies or parts.

Holo-communicator: Handheld device used for talking to others, which can also project a 3D image of their face, if desired.

Holo-tablets: Handheld computers that can project images into the air in a 3D format.

Hover cycle: A motorcycle that hovers instead of having the wheels touching the ground.

Hydroponics: Water processing plant.

Inccukai: Elite assassins that were raised and trained to protect Allied Planetary Union Ambassadors. Some have left the order and taken jobs as freelance bodyguards and mercenaries. Often get their bodies enhanced with tech.

Joseph's balls: Curse slang term frequently used on the Lower Planets.

Klogs: People who lie about who they really are.

Kuargen: Affiliated Wespero territory gang-town.

Lower Planets: Earth and Mars.

Macintosh: Affiliated Wespero territory gang-town.

Marsanium: Iron-based ore mined on Mars and used to build ships.

Mars Racing Commission: Oversight committee that approves and monitors all racing activities on Mars.

Moonie: Slang term for those who live on Earth's moon.

MP: Mars Protectorate.

NiteOx: Deadly fuel-enhancing gas discovered in 2330.

Nkosi: Affiliated Wespero territory gang-town.

Pup: Slang for law enforcement from the Allied Planetary Union (APU).

Recycle: Waste water processed and filtered for human consumption, but not as high quality as pure water.

Rising Sun: Affiliated Wespero territory gang-town.

Runners: Smugglers who run illegal drugs from Earth to other planets.

Scurdy: A scaredy-cat, someone who is afraid.

Skeiron: Affiliated Auster territory gang-town.

Silva-Chavez: Affiliated Wespero territory gang-town.

Singh: Affiliated Wespero territory gang-town.

Slip drives: Primary engines used by space-faring ships, which allow them to travel the currents in space.

Sludge: By-product of processed Marsanium that is used to fuel the racers on Mars.

Space fish: Slang term for someone who travels space, isn't familiar with planetary life or activities and tends to be impressed easily.

Space hole: A derogatory term, another way to say asshole.

Trolling engine: An engine powered by electricity that works in tandem with a ship's slip drive and can be used inside a planet's atmosphere and when moving short distances.

Uni-rider: A motorcycle-style bike that runs off Marsanium sludge.

Upper: A person who lives on an Upper planet.

Upper planets: Jupiter, Saturn and Neptune, including their moons.

Zephyr: Affiliated Auster territory gang-town.

Want to see more from this author? Here's a taster for you to enjoy!

Full Throttle Cyborgs: Too Hemi for You
Landra Graf

Coming May 2023

Excerpt

The weights were heavy, and Hemi Finster was surviving on pure determination not to let Shannon down. *Not that she's coming back.*

Sweat beaded on his forehead, and he grunted as he pushed on the bar driving the round weights at either end upward. The muscles in his human and cybernetic arms burned. He shouldn't have cared so much about a woman he barely knew, but then again, his post-surgery hired nurse had been the only one who didn't treat him like something fragile or broken. *It's their damn fault I'm this way to begin with.*

"You've got this," Gina said on a low note. She shouldn't have needed to be here, but Hemi knew damn well she carried guilt for what happened to him. *More than anyone else does.*

So, when he needed someone to spot him or work beside him in case anything went wrong with his physical therapy since Shannon had left, Gina was always the first to volunteer.

He embraced those words and let out another sound, more like a low roar, as he pushed the weights up. Gina then held the bar with one hand and put it on the hoists.

"Perfect. Great job. That's ten reps today and you're almost not straining. I bet in a week we can move up to thirty pounds on each side. I can get Snapper to bore another hole in a chunk of Marsanium. Not like we're using it for much else besides sludge."

Hemi sat up and took the proffered towel from Gina with his human hand. He refused to voice the truth—that sheer willpower had gotten that last rep in. He'd been so close to letting the weights fall on him. "Let's not rush things."

No, no rushing…because as much as part of him wanted behind the wheel of a racer, another deep-seated voice told him to run. Run as fast as he could to escape whatever the future held or drown himself in drink until he couldn't remember the racer blowing up, his body on fire, then passing out from the agony. The pain had been so acute that sometimes he could swear the nerve endings of the left side of his body were still on fire.

He'd fought against those insidious ideas over and over as he tried to gain control of the new parts on half of his body.

"Of course not." Gina offered a jug of water. "I'm just excited to see you doing so well. You're sticking to the regimen Shannon provided, and even after they've been gone a few days, you're still doing everything she said."

"Yeah." He took a long swallow of water then mopped at his head and neck again with the towel. The fast difference in the experience of moving was upsetting. He could feel the rough, absorbent material of the towel, but the jug in his metal cybernetic hand was a cold nothing.

His life was filled with this half-existence now.

"I'm going to head out since that was the last rep. Promised Snapper I'd help him finish some test runs…"

Gina trailed off, as he couldn't stop staring at his metallic hand gripping the jug, how a slight bit of pressure and he could crush the metal construction. Except he wasn't sure how much strength to use or how long he could last before his hand would fail him.

"Have a good night and tell Snapper I said hello." He tried his best in these moments to summon expected responses, forcing himself to interact with others for the seemingly mundane sense of normalcy.

"What about you?"

"Dinner at the Watering Hole, as usual. Gaia is doing something new tonight, a recipe she got from a traveler. It's something called a dumpling."

"Ooh, yes. I'll remind Snapper. We wanted to try those as well. Maybe we'll see you there."

Hope not.

"Sounds good." He set the jug on the floor and stood, draping the towel around his neck. Gina appeared to believe his movements implied he was in a good enough state to leave.

Her hovering was nice, to a point. But as the metal door to the makeshift workout room clanged shut, he let himself plop back on the workout bench. Everything there, the metal frame, the uprights holding the weight bar and the weights themselves rattled.

His hip ached, and he didn't miss the little bit of dizziness that remained due to his weight differential between the human body remaining and cybernetic components.

He was training to gain extend the stamina of his cybernetic parts, gain control of their strength, and increase his human body mass to offset changes the cybernetic parts exerted.

Fuck. He could easily lay back on the bench and not bother moving, but if Gaia didn't see him walk through the Watering Hole doors in the next hour, she'd send someone to check on him.

He snapped the towel off his neck and tossed it across the room, the only physical manifestation of his frustration.

Full Throttle was the reason he'd been given a shot at being a driver to begin with and without them he wouldn't be alive, which was the thought that propelled him off the bench and to his house. He washed up and avoided looking at himself in the cracked mirror.

A half hour later, Hemi felt as ready to face the crowd in the Watering Hole as he could. He spent a good ten minutes debating on walking with his cane or without. The Marsanium rod in his hand provided a tiny bit of security, just in case.

His stomach growled repeatedly as he made his way to the building. Old wood panels pressure-sealed against metal plating, the wooden boardwalk, the covering and the repainted sign in bright black announced the Watering Hole to anyone who passed by. The wind had died down a bit from earlier so minimal red dust wound through the air, enough so that he didn't need to cover his face. The sunset in the distance cast a deep red glow across the entire town. The buildings looked as if they'd been painted in blood, a visual that brought memories he didn't care to recall.

When he opened the door to the bar, the rush of voices, musical notes, the clink of glasses and laughter hit his ears. Here he could forget about his problems for a minute as those from the gang who gathered were rather good at focusing conversation elsewhere. He basked in the smell of hops and wheat brews along with mouth-watering spices and the heavy scent of yeasty bread.

"Hemi, you made it before I had to send a minder," Gaia called out to him as she filled two mugs with house brew and passed them off to one of her helpers.

"You mean a minion? What did I say about needing regular checkups?"

"My workers are always happy to escape for a minute during the evening rush, so think of it as doing them a favor."

A favor, my ass. He warred between appreciating the gesture and hating the threat to his independence with a passion. Since the accident, he'd barely been left alone, yet here he was deliberately seeking out a busy place because drowning his veins in alcohol appeared the best way to stave off the nightmares that might creep up on him.

"Here's the stew with the dumplings. If you want more, just ask. And the brew." Gaia set down a mug and bowl with a wood-carved spoon. "Enjoy."

Then she was gone, the long, pale blonde braid of hers swinging as she turned and moved to the next customer at the bar. Though that was where Frog Lick differed from every other gangtown. No one had to pay, even non-gang member customers. Food and brew were always free if a person was in the bar. Money didn't exchange hands unless someone wanted something other than house brew, usually recycle or any type of alcohol with more bite.

Drag, their fearless leader, believed in giving sustenance to everyone in town. No one deserved to starve, ever. The community, the gang, lifted each other up. Free food for anyone. Where some of the larger, stout members might have been greedy in other gangs, eating three to five servings of anything they could have, people in Frog Lick never took more than two servings, to help ensure there was enough to go around.

Hemi grabbed his items and moved away from the bar to clear space for the next set of arrivals. Usually, he sat up front near the stage, listening to the music from the local guitarist, Privy. But tonight, he opted for a table closer to the door. After the long day, he wanted to eat and drink, then get out.

Snapper and Gina most likely wouldn't show. Drag was out with his brother, Rune, and Petal, Rune's wife. Jack... well, Jack and Hemi's hired nurse were off on a mission to save him and his fellow cyborgs.

Chasing solutions to cybernetic degradation. I was saved just to be destroyed again.

That supported the idea of having another drink instead of rushing home. Who knew if Jack and Shannon would even be successful? If they weren't, his days were numbered, and he'd much rather spend them in distraction.

"Hi, Hemi." One of the many single Frog Lick ladies slid an arm around his shoulders, while another sat in the chair beside him.

Both women wore grins and a provocative glint lit their eyes. That was about where their similarities ended. Josie, with her auburn hair and her freckle-covered skin, and Haimea, with her rich black waves and dark sienna tones, were the exact opposites of each other in every way, except they were both hardcore dust honeys.

"You're looking good. Maybe those cybernetic parts will help in the next race?"

He wouldn't be behind the wheel any time soon. "Maybe. What brings you lovely ladies to my table?"

The pair glanced at each and then at him. He tried to take all of their admiration in stride, tried to pretend he enjoyed Haimea snaking her tattooed hand across his pant-covered cybernetic thigh, though he couldn't feel a thing. Therein lay the problem — even though these ladies continually offered themselves to him, Hemi couldn't bring himself to disappoint them. In times past, he'd enjoyed the sexual overtures of both ladies and even their sensual enthusiasm. They found pleasure with each other as much as they seemed to delight in sharing him.

"We were thinking it's been a while since you had us over."

"Uh-huh." Josie leaned in closer with her lips at his ear, her red locks draping over his shoulder. "We miss that delicious mouth of yours."

They missed what he could do for them, but he wasn't capable of such things anymore. At least not in the sense of full involvement. It was fully possible to engage in the use of his mouth without other parts of his anatomy. If he truly wanted a distraction, they would provide it.

"Well, I'm happy for a reunion."

"That's not all we want…"

Josie kept talking, but Hemi found himself distracted by the opening of the Water Hole door. It creaked as it was spread wide, lingering sunlight from the setting sun shining into the darker room, a haze of red dust kicked up. For a second, it looked like the entrance was on fire. Then she walked in, pale blonde hair whipping around a slender tanned neck, greenish blue eyes that reminded him of the saturated chem pools the Uppers drowning in flash swam in. He'd even known a person who had one. She had the same look, same graceful walk, same — *Fuck.*

And just like that, his past had walked in the door. Hemi stumbled to a standing position, unsure if he should run toward a woman who always seemed to turn up in his life at the wrong time to hug her close and thank whatever higher power existed.

But as fast as she appeared, she whisked right back out the door and it slammed shut.

Hemi was still in a state of shock, eyes blinking rapidly and wondering if he'd seen a mirage or if this was the start of the degradation. "Ladies, I think I may need to call it a night. We can pick this up tomorrow."

Both women pouted, their lips dusted in a pink glitter that reflected tiny sparks at the slightest hint of light. He had no desire to appease them and whatever distraction he'd hoped to find was lost in the minute he'd dreamed of seeing a part of his past.

"You promise?"

He did his best to summon a grin that would rival the way he used to smile at the women. "Have I broken one yet? Tomorrow."

They both came to either side of him and pressed their lips against his cheeks, leaving their mark, before giggling and walking off to find the next male driver or mechanic willing to entertain them. Though drivers were slim picking with Jack gone and Drag retired — he was the last one.

And there's not much left.

He pounded back the rest of his beer, left the empty mug on the table then headed for the door. Once on the porch, he turned to the left using his cane to help support his weight. Since he'd been sitting, his human side was even more worn out than earlier. The trip to his makeshift home, the one Drag had gifted him when he'd joined up with Full Throttle, would probably take longer than it should. Though home wasn't the same without — *her*.

This time she had a hood on, but he didn't miss those eyes or the way her long, pale blonde hair cascaded over her shoulders, the sensuous yet agile way she moved. He'd often likened her to an angel with tanned skin and a piercing gaze that could either make one melt or wither.

"Hemi?"

His name sounded more like a question from her lips. He was so screwed. It looked like his past had just caught up to him, and it wasn't leaving without a reckoning.

About the Author

Landra Graf consumes at least one book a day, and has always been a sucker for stories where true love conquers all. She believes in the power of the written word, and the joy such words can bring. In between spending time with her family and having book adventures, she writes romance with the goal of giving everyone, fictional or not, their own happily ever after.

Landra loves to hear from readers. You can find her contact information, website details and author profile page at https://www.totallybound.com

Home of Erotic Romance

Sign up for our newsletter and find out about all our romance book releases, eBook sales and promotions, sneak peeks and FREE romance books!